From *The New York Times*:

"Since many folk tales are anonymous and ever changing, Charles Sullivan has done the retelling of what he calls the most interesting American tales. . . . Sullivan writes with a relaxed, modern tone ('easy come, easy go,' as Jesse James used to say) but never slangy. Although he skillfully slips in details of history and geography, he also conveys a sense of spirit and energy."

UNCLE SAM'S FAMILY

STORIES OF EXCEPTIONAL AMERICANS AND THEIR AMAZING ANIMALS

CHARLES SULLIVAN

Uncle Sam's Family:
Stories of Exceptional Americans and Their Amazing Animals

Published by Kezaco

Copyright © 2012 Charles Sullivan

For more information, email the publisher:
kezaco@earthlink.net

Book design by Maureen Cutajar
Cover design by Tatiana Vila

ISBN: 978-0-9855411-1-8

CONTENTS

UNCLE SAM'S FAMILY

AMERICA'S FIRST "UNCLE SAM"

Samuel G. Wilson was nobody's hero, not even his own. Although he worked for a small company that supplied meat to the United States Army during the 1840s, he had never been near any fighting. Sam was a patriotic young man, however, and when the war with Mexico erupted in 1846, he felt he had to help. So he started writing cheerful messages on the smooth wooden barrels of salted pork and beef as he packed them for shipment.

"Greetings to U.S. soldiers," he'd say, using heavy black crayon, "from yr. loyal friend Sam'l. Wilson of Troy, New York."

After repeating this message dozens of times he decided to have a little more fun with it, so he signed himself "yr. loving uncle Sam Wilson," even though he was no older than most of the troops.

One day Sam received a wrinkled letter that had come all the way from a military post office at Galveston, Texas.

"Dear Uncle Sam," the letter said. "We may not make it home alive from this blamed neck o' the woods, but here's eight of us soljers got no other relatives on the face of the earth, so to you Uncle we say 'Thankee' for yr good food & kind words." Six signatures followed, plus two Xs and then a P.S. "We're wondering what do you look like?"

Sam Wilson looked like many another young man: light brown hair, medium height, slightly on the heavy side of average weight. He assumed the soldiers would rather have a more interesting Uncle, however, so he walked around his town on the Fourth of July, studying the flags and decorations, listening to people talk. After much thought, he had an idea about how to reply to that letter from Texas.

"I'm a lean and sinewy old fellow," he wrote, "with long white hair and white chin whiskers, eyes of fiercest blue, and a nose like the prow of a fighting ship. My favorite pantaloons are striped red and white, and my blue swallowtail coat has white stars on it. My tall hat has stars on it too. I love these United States more dearly than the bald eagle loves his chicks. I've got fists hard as rocks but fingers that can play a fiddle faster than most of you could dance. My temper is a lot hotter than a grizzly bear's, yet I can be as cool as a cucumber when there's danger. Though I tend to be gentle with those weaker than myself, I can honestly swear to you that I've never run from a battle nor lost a fight."

As a matter of fact, young Sam Wilson had never won a fight, either, and he hadn't ever been in a battle anywhere, but he saw no point in saying so. He added a few more paragraphs of fanciful details and mailed this letter off to his eight homesick "nephews" near the Mexican border.

Several weeks later he happened to see a newspaper from Albany, New York, with a headline that pulled him up short.

"UNCLE SAM VISITS U.S. TROOPS IN TEXAS," it said. Underneath the headline was a drawing very much like the imaginary character he had described in his letter, and a long story about Uncle Sam cheering up the American soldiers.

"He walked among us like a giant among midgets," an excited young Army corporal from Rhode Island was quoted as saying, "and behind him a thousand American banners sprang up like red, white, and blue flowers." Other soldiers made similar statements, full of wild enthusiasm. Reading these words, Sam Wilson feared that his creation, "Uncle Sam," had gotten out of hand. What should he do about it? "For one thing, I'd better quit writing messages on meat barrels," he decided. "Nothing but plain old 'U.S. Army' from now on."

But he saw more newspaper stories about Uncle Sam as time went by, and he began to realize that, wherever this thing might be going, it was out of his control now. Even after the Mexican War ended in 1848, Uncle Sam kept popping up in other places, at home and abroad, and when the Civil War broke out in 1861, Uncle Sam appeared to be supporting both sides. Confederate soldiers talked about him and wrote letters, while Yankees were still claiming him for their own.

Year after year, so many new "nephews" and also some young "nieces" responded to this colorful creation that Samuel Wilson felt no need to raise a real family of his own. He often visited the homes of his younger brothers and sisters, however, and he loved it when their children addressed him as "Uncle Sam."

Angelo Buys a Goose

It was the week after Christmas, December 1899, and the island of Manhattan lay covered by a sparkling crust of snow that was freezing harder as the sun set. A young businessman named Angelo Fortunato, walking swiftly home to his new wife, Louisa, laughed like a schoolboy as he skidded and slid on the icy pavement. Other houses looked inviting, to be sure, but they could not compare with his! Candles in the front windows, green holly wreath on the door, sand sprinkled where the steps might be slippery: everything just right, thanks to Louisa!

He rushed inside to embrace her—blonde, a little stout in her build, very pretty, smiling at him. . . no, she was not smiling this time. Frowning, it seemed.

"What's the matter, my darling?" he cried, still cheerful.

"Tomorrow night is New Year's Eve," she replied, looking at him oddly.

"Indeed it is, my precious."

"And tonight you were supposed to bring me a goose."

"Goose?" he repeated. "Goose for what?"

"Goose for New Year's dinner, of course."

"But in my family, Louisa, we've always had turkey and ham."

"In my family we've always had goose," she responded, as if that would settle the matter.

And so it did, as far as Angelo was concerned, for he adored Louisa. They had been married less than a year, and he found great satisfaction in doing things to please her. Get a goose for New Year's dinner? Why not! He vaguely remembered a farmers' market on Staten Island, with live white geese for sale.

"I know just the place to get one," he assured her, but Louisa scarcely heard him, for now she was busy putting tonight's supper on the table—fat German sausages, mashed potatoes and gravy, carrots cooked with their tops on: one of his favorite meals. He sat down to eat, and Louisa hovered a moment before joining him. She was just as eager to please her new husband as he was to please her.

"Delicious!" he exclaimed, and they both smiled.

The next day Angelo closed his waterfront office early, wished his clerks a Happy New Year, and rode the trolley line to the tip of Manhattan where he could catch a ferryboat across the harbor to Staten Island. A chilly wind made the water choppy, but Angelo found the weather invigorating. He hadn't taken this boat ride in years, so he was one of the few passengers who stood outside despite the cold, seeing the huge Statue of Liberty and other sights as though for the first time. How wonderful! Just before the ferryboat docked, Angelo glanced back at the distant skyline of lower Manhattan, and tried to picture Louisa at that moment. Sewing, perhaps, or she might be reading. Louisa was a great reader.

"I'd do anything for her!" he thought. "Well, almost anything."

Stepping off the boat, Angelo asked for directions to the farmers' market. Four miles to walk; a bit more than he had remembered, but he was in the prime of life and he felt that he could do it easily, even with fresh snow on the ground.

Striding along, Angelo whistled cheerfully as he recalled the events of the past year: meeting Louisa at a party, falling rapidly and deliriously in love with her, getting the sweetest hints that she might love him, too, then meeting her parents, proposing marriage, being accepted, buying a new suit for the wedding. . . .

Angelo was too busy with these memories to notice that he had taken a wrong turn in the gathering dusk. Suddenly he realized that he was walking past a lonely row of boarded-up houses, almost a deserted village. But he could see lights ahead, and hear people talking, so he pushed on until he found them.

Beyond the houses, several wagons had stopped where two country lanes crossed, and men he took to be local farmers were transacting business of some kind by lantern light. Approaching them, Angelo saw that one man was holding a pair of noisy white geese in his arms.

"Excuse me," Angelo said, "but I would like very much to buy a goose for dinner."

"These two are sold already," the farmer replied.

"Do you have others, perhaps?" Angelo persisted.

"Well, I've got a Canada goose I could sell you," said the farmer, nodding towards his wagon, "but she may not be exactly what you want."

"What's a Canada goose?"

"Good-sized bird, mostly brown and white feathers, lots of solid meat on her," the farmer replied. "She must have been in one of them big V's of geese flying south for the Winter, but she hurt her wing some way, and landed in my pond two months ago. Here, have a look at her."

Angelo examined the goose, and made his decision.

"I'll take her," he said.

They agreed on the price, which seemed fair enough, and the farmer drove away. Anglelo tried to carry the goose under his arm, but the big bird was too heavy for him. However, she seemed quite willing to accompany him on foot, so Angelo walked back down the dark country lane with the Canada goose waddling beside him. As he passed the closed-up houses again, he caught a whiff of wood-smoke on the wind, and wondered who might be living in this lonely place.

Suddenly a door opened and a nasty-looking man lurched out onto the road, grabbing Angelo by the shoulder.

"Here he is!" the fellow shouted to others inside. "Coming to bring us our New Year's goose now, isn't he?"

Angelo twisted away from the man's heavy grip. Courteously but firmly, he explained that the goose was meant for nobody but his wife, and he must hurry home. At first the man tried to bargain with him, blocking his path.

"Give you half a gallon of the best hard cider you ever did taste," the man said. "Give you two half a gallon; two halves of a gallon," he offered, as Angelo continued to refuse.

"Well, I guess we'll just have to take your goose, then, won't we?" said the man, turning nasty again.

He pushed Angelo into the house, where three other rough-looking men were sitting on the floor near a glowing wood-stove, playing cards. They stood up quickly to join in this new game, and Angelo felt scared: nobody there to help him, nothing to defend himself with. As the ruffians advanced, he backed slowly into the farthest corner of the empty room. Beside him, the goose started hissing at their foes. When one of them got too close, the goose struck swiftly with her beak, and the fellow leaped away. Again he tried, and the angry goose drove him back, striking at arm or leg, as the other rascals watched. Angelo felt a surge of hope, but there were four of them against him; this couldn't go on much longer.

He looked around desperately and saw something in the corner, a crude wooden rake with broken teeth and a long handle. Not much of a weapon, but better than nothing! Angelo picked it up and held it high, ready to swing at them.

"Let me go peacefully with my goose," he said loudly, "or I will have to hurt you."

The four men laughed at that, drew knives from under their coats, and edged closer to him. Instead of retreating, however, Angelo swung his weapon furiously, whacking anyone he could reach. Whack! Whack! Whack!

Angelo's goose stood beside him, hissing and striking with her beak. Ouch! Ouch! Ouch!

Three of the ruffians ran out of the house. The meanest one remained, slashing with his knife left, right, left again, so close that Angelo could see the fierce red light of rage in his eyes. But Angelo wasn't frightened any more! With his goose at his side he was advancing now, yelling at the wicked fellow and whacking him, through the open doorway and out into the lane.

"I told you (Whack!) this goose is for my dear wife (Whack!) and I'm going (Whack!) to take it (Whack!) to her now" (Whack! Whack!).

Angelo and his goose stood together in the lane, watching the last of the defeated ruffians slink away. The night was dark, but the winter moon had climbed higher in the sky, and Angelo had no difficulty finding his way back to the ferry dock, the big goose walking beside him.

When he finally got home, Angelo embraced his dear wife even more warmly than usual. But what should he say? He hesitated to tell her that he didn't have the heart to kill his brave goose.

"What's that wonderful smell?" he asked.

"A ham I'm baking for tomorrow," Louisa replied.

"Ham? I thought you wanted goose."

"No, my dear," she explained. "After you left I realized I was being selfish. If ham and turkey are what you want for dinner, then ham and turkey you shall have."

So Angelo and his wife celebrated New Year's Day together, with pleasure, and many another holiday after that.

Angelo's goose took up residence in their small back yard, guarding the house whenever they were out. She seemed contented enough for the rest of that Winter, but as Spring approached she scanned the sky more and more often.

One fine morning, her injury fully mended, the goose honked loudly at Angelo as he came out of the house. He whistled to her fondly, and fed her a few kernels of corn. She honked again. Then she spread her mighty wings, took off easily, and flew up to join the V's of other big Canada geese, all flying rapidly towards the north.

BLACK BART THE STAGECOACH ROBBER

A man who called himself "Charles E. Boles" taught school in a California mining town during the early 1870s, when gold could still be found by those willing to dig deep enough for it. Boles was a slim, quiet, neatly dressed individual who kept mostly to himself, yet every once in a while he surprised people with his big toothy smile and his unexpected displays of humor.

He just loved to play practical jokes. Not on any of his students, but almost anybody else: another teacher, or a friend or acquaintance, sometimes even a total stranger. He always looked dignified and serious while he carefully prepared the surprise. Then, as his victim realized it must be a joke, Boles would burst into loud laughter, slapping his thighs, whooping and hollering like a man gone crazy.

One day his joking went too far. Boles was riding home after school, guiding his gray horse along a rough trail that crossed the main road, when he saw a red and yellow Wells Fargo stagecoach coming slowly up the mountain. He recognized the man who was driving, and thought it would be fun to scare him a little. So Boles hid his horse behind some mesquite shrubs, broke off a crooked stick to pretend he had a pistol, tied a bandana over his mouth for a mask, and stepped out into the road as the stage approached. It stopped abruptly.

"Throw down your moneybox!" Boles shouted.

The driver, startled and frightened, did just that, and the heavy metal box burst open when it hit the ground beside the road, spilling out golden bars and several canvas sacks of gold dust. No telling how much all of this might be worth! As Boles stood there, forgetting to reveal who he was, the driver yelled at the horses and the stagecoach rolled away.

Bart started packing the gold back into the box, thinking he could catch up with the stagecoach and explain his joke to the driver and passengers. But then he thought some more. Even if he continued to teach school for many years, he couldn't earn nearly as much money as this treasure was worth right now; why not just keep it? Stealing was wrong, of course, but remaining poor didn't seem to be exactly the right idea either. Boles quickly stuffed the gold into his saddlebags and rode off, leaving the empty Wells Fargo box behind. Thus began his new and exciting career as a bandit.

When he got home to his rented wooden shanty, Boles did what a lot of people in those parts did: he pried up one of the floorboards to make a hiding place. Down there he placed one small sack of gold dust, an old watch that lacked a minute hand, and various other odds and ends of no great value. He was tempted to add some kind of a funny note for any robber who might come along, but then he supposed it might be better to leave well enough alone. The rest of the gold he buried out in the brush at several different locations, which he memorized before doing another thing.

During the next seven years, Charles Boles held up more than thirty Wells Fargo stagecoaches, mostly in California's mountainous "gold country" where he knew every turn of the roads. Some drivers were braver than others, some stages carried armed guards as well, but Boles always managed to take them by surprise, usually at a spot where the stage was going slowly, climbing a steep grade or starting to cross a stream. He never fired a shot, and never got caught. Well, almost never; detectives from Wells Fargo did catch up with him, but that was later on.

Compared to other outlaws, Boles was probably luckier and smarter than most. He planned every detail in advance, and was careful about disguising himself and hiding his tracks. But he could never resist a joke. After each robbery of a stagecoach, he would leave a humorous note in the empty moneybox. For example:

"This is my way to get money and bread.
When I have a chance, why should I refuse it?
I'll not need either when I'm dead,
And I only tax those who are able to lose it.

"So blame me not for what I've done,
I don't deserve your curses;
And if for some cause I must be hung,
Let it be for my verses."

Boles signed each of these poetic notes with a name that was also meant to be a joke, "Black Bart, the Po-8."

Not long after Black Bart the poet began holding up Wells Fargo stagecoaches, Mr. Charles E. Boles the schoolteacher quit his job and quickly disappeared from the mining community where he had been working. Coincidentally a prosperous and well-dressed gentleman who used the name "C. E. Bolton" arrived in San Francisco, and let it be known that his prosperity came from several goldmines up in the mountains, which he had to visit periodically. Nobody connected Bolton with Boles, or either one of those two with Black Bart, and it was only by chance that the poetry-writing bandit was finally caught. The vital clue to his identity was discovered because of the brave actions of a fifteen-year-old boy named Jimmy Roleri.

On a cool November day in 1883, near the Stanislaus River in California's central valley, Black Bart held up the stagecoach in which Jimmy Roleri was coming back from a visit to his grandparents. When Bart suddenly appeared out of nowhere, waving his gun, the driver threw down the moneybox without a fight, but this time it didn't break open right away.

Smash! Bart attacked the box, using the sledgehammer and chisel that he always carried with him just in case. Splintering the lid, he kicked it aside.

The box was partly full of gold, as usual, and Bart lost no time loading it into the saddlebags on his nearby horse. He needed only two or three minutes to do all of this. Then he put his usual note in the moneybox and climbed onto his horse.

When Jimmy Roleri realized what was happening, he slipped out the far side of the coach and crouched behind it, taking the new .22-caliber single-shot rifle he had been given for his birthday. Just as Black Bart was about to ride away, Jimmy aimed the rifle and fired his one shot.

Bart was hit in the arm or hand. He lost his black derby hat as he galloped off. And a detachable white cuff, spotted with blood, fell from the sleeve of his shirt.

At last the detectives who worked for Wells Fargo, led by an expert named James Hume, had a couple of clues to follow. The derby hat didn't help much, because they couldn't tell who might have owned it. But the shirt cuff, made of best white linen, had been marked "F.X.0.7" by a commercial laundry somewhere to identify a particular customer. Find that laundry and they would have their man!

More than three dozen Wells Fargo detectives spread out across the rugged landscape of the "gold country," looking for the laundry that had marked someone's shirt that way. No luck in the mining towns, where most people did their own washing, or did without. No luck in nearby cities such as Placerville or Sacramento, where the Chinese laundry workers always marked things in their own language.

So the detectives spread out further, some going as far as Las Vegas and Los Angeles. Finally, in San Francisco, the detectives found a laundry that recognized the "F.X.0.7" mark and identified their customer: Mr. C. E. Bolton, who resided at an elegant private hotel, the Webb House, not far away.

The rest was easy. Having stationed several of his best men along the hallway and downstairs beneath the windows, chief detective Hume knocked on the door of Bolton's hotel suite, carrying a bundle of clean shirts from the laundry, as though he were making a delivery. When Bolton started to pay him, Hume interrupted.

"I think this may also be yours, Bart."

Hume handed him the blood-spotted shirt cuff that had led the detectives to him. Bart was surprised of course, and scared; but he had to laugh too, because this time the joke was on him.

Bolton/Bart/Boles served six years in San Quentin prison for armed robbery. That brought an end to his poetry, but his story wasn't quite finished. Indeed, there are several different accounts of what Black Bart did in his later years. Let's pick one and follow it to the end.

Soon after Bart was released from prison, a masked bandit began holding up the few Wells Fargo stagecoaches that still carried gold down from the mines in the mountains. Each time this robber took the stage drivers by surprise, never firing a shot, and each time he managed to get away. Though the shipments were much lighter and less frequent than they had been before, there was still enough gold in the moneyboxes for a patient, experienced bandit to make a living.

No funny notes were left in the boxes now, and no more poetry, but the Wells Fargo detectives were fairly sure they knew who was doing these robberies. So they searched for him again in San Francisco, found him pretty easily, and had a friendly chat. Bart told them he wasn't getting any younger. Actually he would like to retire from this line of work, if he could be assured of enough money to live on.

"How about a monthly payment from the company?" he asked.

Black Bart may have meant this as a joke, but the detectives took it seriously. Three days later, Wells Fargo decided to pay him a comfortable little pension each month for the rest of his life, if he would solemnly promise to stop robbing them. Bart gave his word, shook hands on the deal, and that was the end of his story.

Br'er Rabbit Meets Br'er Fox

Back in the days when small animals roamed freely through the pathless woods and flowering fields of rural Georgia, they were usually peaceable. Rabbits, squirrels, chipmunks, raccoons, possums, and other creatures thought of themselves as one big family. They called each other "Brother" and "Sister" when they happened to meet, while looking for food in the underbrush or getting a drink of water at the creek. Of course Br'er Rabbit might disagree with Br'er Possum about something, now and then, or Sis' Squirrel might scold her naughty youngsters, or several Raccoons might try to take a meal away from Crows. But most of the time, there were no serious conflicts.

This all changed years ago, as families of red foxes moved down into Georgia from Virginia and the Carolinas to get away from angry farmers, especially those who raised chickens or ducks. Most of Georgia was still wide open; there were miles of meadows and pinewoods where foxes could go hunting to their hearts' content. And Georgia's soft clay soil was perfect for digging burrows that were snug to live in and easy to defend. So the red foxes quickly adapted to their new environment; they forced other animals to change. Since foxes preferred to hunt at night, the raccoons and possums stayed hidden then, and did their own hunting during the daylight hours. Rabbits bunched together in huge colonies that foxes hesitated to attack. Chipmunks and squirrels shifted their nests from the ground into the trees, building new homes high among the swaying boughs where no fox could climb. Crows and smaller birds served as lookouts, warning all the creatures on the ground when a fox showed up. Every animal did something to help.

Every animal, that is, except one: the brown, furry rascal with long floppy ears, a wiggly nose, and a rather quick, sometimes mischievous mind. He called himself "Br'er Rabbit," like thousands of rabbits in that part of Georgia, but he was prouder, more self-assured, and possibly smarter than most of the others. He wasn't about to run from any number of red foxes, and he refused to huddle with rest of the rabbits in crowded, frightened communities.

Br'er Rabbit had created his own comfortable home, deep inside a seemingly impenetrable thicket of thorny wild roses, with delicious perfume surrounding him, and the gentle humming of bees. And he had improved his natural defenses with sharp-pointed quills given to him by Br'er Porcupine, some pungent musk from Br'er Skunk, and certain other tricks and surprises he kept to himself.

Though his life had been pleasant and safe enough, up to this point, Br'er Rabbit did have a problem or two. He wasn't quite as alert as he should have been, so he stumbled into trouble at times. And because he didn't socialize much with other animals, he didn't always get the latest warnings. Therefore Br'er Rabbit wasn't aware that a new enemy had moved into the forest nearby. This was a fox: not just your ordinary red fox, but a sly old fellow with gray fur, a gray top hat, and a shiny pair of eyeglasses that he had found somewhere else. He looked like a city slicker, out of place in the Georgia countryside, and that's what he was.

This impressive stranger called himself "Br'er Fox," though the other animals weren't sure he really deserved such a familiar, good-ole-boy name. Living by his wits, and using the lessons learned from a lifetime's experience, he managed to keep himself fat and sassy. His new life in Georgia was not very exciting for Br'er Fox, however, so when he heard that his neighbors included a solitary rabbit that might be more clever than most, he became very interested. At last, he thought: the possibility of a worthy opponent for me to play with! Br'er Fox spent the afternoon making special preparations, then took a long snooze in his underground burrow while he waited for this particular rabbit to appear.

Awakened by the pit-pat, pittery-pat of footsteps, Br'er Fox peeked out as Br'er Rabbit hopped lightly along a path that zigzagged through the woods from his home to his favorite patch of purple cabbages. Br'er Rabbit was wearing a child's blue coveralls and a straw hat with holes for his oversized ears. Br'er Fox had never seen a rabbit wearing human clothes before. However, he figured that one rabbit probably tasted as good as another, clothes or no clothes, so he pulled a string that he had arranged earlier, and suddenly a tar-baby stood up in the path.

Tar-baby? This was nothing more than a good-sized doll made of sticks covered with tar, and a cotton diaper covering its middle, but Br'er Rabbit had never seen such a thing before. He stopped and stared at it.

"What do you want?" he asked the tar-baby.

Br'er Fox chuckled in the bushes, for he knew what he wanted, sure enough, while the tar-baby was silent.

"Do you want something?" Br'er Rabbit persisted. "If not, stand aside and let me pass."

The tar-baby remained silent.

"I'll just be on my way, then," Br'er Rabbit said.

He tried to squeeze past the tar-baby without touching it, but the path was too narrow. Br'er Fox, still hiding, jerked his string again and the tar-baby fell heavily against Br'er Rabbit, getting sticky black tar all over his blue coveralls.

"Where are you going?" Br'er Rabbit cried. "Watch what you're doing!"

He moved this way and that, but the tar-baby swung around and stayed close to him, so that Br'er Rabbit got smeared with more and more of the smelly, sticky tar, whichever way he turned. His blue coveralls were now ruined, and the brim of his straw hat was also smeared with tar. Angrily, Br'er Rabbit pushed against the tar-baby with both front paws to move him out of the way. But he only got stuck deeper in the tar.

"I'll show him," Br'er Rabbit thought, and launched some mighty kicks at the tar-baby with his strong back legs. But now his back paws got stuck in the tar, and he fell to the ground, rolling over and over, struggling to get up. He couldn't do it. The harder he tried, the worse it was. Finally he lay on the ground, panting, worn out, looking more like a tar-baby than the tar-baby itself. Only then did Br'er Fox emerge from the bushes, bowing and smirking at his helpless captive.

"Good afternoon, Brother Rabbit," he said smoothly. "How nice of you to accept my invitation for dinner."

Dinner? Whose dinner? As upset as he was, Br'er Rabbit sensed that he was in great danger, and he immediately started thinking about how to get away. He was pretty smart himself. But could he outfox this sly old villain? After a pause he replied.

"Just being neighborly, Brother Fox," he said, "just being neighborly to a newcomer. I'll be happy to dine with you this evening. But I'm a tad early, so I'll just hop along home, change my clothes, clean myself up, and be back with you directly."

"You need not put yourself to so much trouble, Brother," said Br'er Fox. "This meal is going to be real casual. Just the two of us. And since you seem to be having trouble walking now, I'll just pull you along by the ears."

That turned out to be quite uncomfortable for Br'er Rabbit, as Br'er Fox hauled him through the bushes towards his burrow, but there was no use in complaining.

"Anything you say, Brother Fox," said Br'er Rabbit, "anything you say is fine and dandy with me, but please—"

He paused, and Br'er Fox waited politely.

"Please," Br'er Rabbit went on, "whatever you do, please don't throw me into that awful briar patch, over yonder to your left."

Br'er Fox, still unfamiliar with much of country life, didn't see how getting thrown into a big briar patch could be more painful than getting cooked for rabbit stew. But he had a cruel streak in his nature, like many foxes, and the idea of this tar-streaked young rabbit squirming and suffering rather pleased him.

"Are you positive you wouldn't like me to throw you in there, tar and all?" he asked

"Ab-so-tee-totally positive," Br'er Rabbit assured him. "I couldn't think of anything worse."

Hearing this, Br'er Fox swung Br'er Rabbit back and forth several times, then hurled him through the air into the middle of the briar patch, where he disappeared among roses and thorns.

"Ouch! Ouch!" shouted Br'er Rabbit, pretending to be badly hurt as he activated his special defenses. "Oh, it hurts something dreadful! I'm bleeding all over! Please come and save me, Mr. Fox!"

Fearing that his rabbit dinner might be spoiled, Br'er Fox found what seemed to be an entrance into the briar patch. He plunged forward, only to stop short as porcupine quills hit him in the nose and raked his sides. Skunk's musk enveloped him with its clinging, sickening aroma. Thorns tore at him, whichever way he tried to move, and something like a snake hissed beneath him, then struck quickly at his unprotected belly. Even the bees that had been a-buzzing in the background came crowding close to him now, and stung his body in a hundred different places.

When he finally succeeded in turning around, Br'er Fox crawled painfully out of the briar patch, leaving his gray hat and his eyeglasses behind as he ran yelping through the woods. He was the first gray fox ever to be seen in that part of Georgia, and also the last.

An hour or so later, after the bees had resumed their pleasant humming, Br'er Rabbit went hip-hop, hippity-hopping down to the creek, where some of the other small animals were gathered.

"What sort of a critter was that nasty old gray thing?" Sis Possum asked, as she helped Br'er Rabbit to clean himself up.

"Some type of a fox, maybe, or a coyote," he replied.

"Whatever," she continued. "It was right neighborly of you to run him out of here, Br'er Rabbit, and we thank you kindly for taking the trouble to do it."

Casey Jones Wrecks a Train

John Luther Jones, known as "Casey" because he came from Casey, Kentucky, was a high-spirited boy who grew up to be a cheerful giant of a man: six feet four and a half inches tall in his bright yellow socks. He began working as an assistant conductor on the Illinois Central Railroad at an early age, and educated himself by asking questions of older men who knew everything about running trains.

Presently he got promoted to the job of conductor, and later to the top job of train driver, or "engineer." He became famous among railroad men for driving his trains to their final destinations on schedule. This may not seem like much of an accomplishment now, but back in Casey's time, the 1890s, it was very difficult to do. Locomotives frequently broke down, tracks were torn up or flooded, switches froze, and other things happened so that trains were usually late when they started out. And often they lost more time as they went along. So the test of a good engineer was how much of the lost time he could make up before reaching the end of the run. Casey Jones got to be very skillful at this, better than any other "train-driving man." His skill, success, and plain old luck would have made him a legend even if he hadn't died young.

The last chapter of his story began around midnight on April 29, 1900. Casey had just driven a freight train into the big railroad yards at Memphis, Tennessee, when he heard that a friend of his was sick, and would not be able to drive another freight that should have left at 11:35 p.m. Nobody else was available on short notice, so Casey offered to drive that train, and his favorite "fireman," Sim Webb, came along to shovel the coal. Sim, one of the secrets of Casey's success up to that point, was a powerful black man who had worked with him for years.

That foggy night, Casey and Sim had to get from Memphis to Canton, Mississippi, more than two hundred miles, through country flooded by two weeks of steady rain. Because of all the delays, their train pulled out of the Memphis yards 90 minutes behind schedule. Normally it would have taken at least five hours to reach the end of the line. They were going to try to do it in three and a half hours, non-stop.

Casey drove the train hard, his right hand on the throttle to regulate speed, his left hand on a cord that released steam from the engine to blow a warning whistle. His special tune was a loud, mournful sound that rose like a trumpet solo as the train rushed along, then died away. That night, making up for so much lost time, he played it often.

While Casey drove, one eye on the clock, Sim fed coal into the train's engine, shoveling faster than he ever had before. Sim too was watching the clock. Later he recalled how rapidly they had been catching up with the schedule, as their long freight train flew past country towns in the quiet hours before dawn.

Sardis, Mississippi, 72 minutes behind schedule.

Grenada, 45 minutes behind.

Winona, 34 minutes.

Durant, 16 minutes.

And soon they were approaching Vaughan, Mississippi, less than seven minutes late. Sim and Casey grinned, and relaxed for just a moment. At this rate, they would pass the next station on time, and pull into Canton bang on schedule.

As their train sped around a sharp curve at Vaughan, however, Casey and Sim yelled at each other. Another train was stopped dead on the track ahead of them. Nobody is quite sure why, to this day. The last car of that train was a caboose, a kind of cabin on wheels where members of the crew could eat and sleep when they weren't on duty. It stood there unlighted, maybe empty, maybe not.

Casey slammed on the brakes and blew his whistle again, but it was impossible to stop in time.

"Jump, Sim, save yourself!" he cried.

Sim dove into the darkness, rolled down an embankment, hit his head and passed out, just as the noise of the terrible crash rolled over him.

Cars of both trains were derailed, the empty caboose was shattered, Casey's locomotve exploded, and Casey himself was killed instantly. Just six minutes short of arriving on time at his final station.

Sim Webb and a man from the other train lived to tell this story of Casey Jones and the train wreck. Later it became a poem, which was set to music and passed along from one train crew to the next. They loved it because it was about them, as well as him:

"Headaches and heartaches and all kinds of pain
Are not apart from a railroad train;
Tales that are earnest, noble and gran'
Belong to the life of a railroad man."

CINDERELLA OF SANTA FE

Once upon a time there was a pretty girl named Gertrudes de Barcelo, who lived with her father and stepmother in the humblest of neighborhoods in Santa Fe, New Mexico. Gertrudes planned to become a princess, just as soon as she had saved enough money to leave home. This was no dream. Day or night, Gertrudes thought about taking the Trailways bus to Palm Beach, Florida, and marrying a prince! She had found magazine articles about Miami, Tucson, Lake Tahoe, and other resorts, but Palm Beach was the home of the young man who appealed to her most: Leland J. Costello, the Fourth. She cut out pictures of him and kept them in a scrapbook.

Falling asleep at night, Gertrudes imagined her first date with the prince she had chosen for herself. He was tall, gentle, handsome. A curly lock of black hair fell across his brown eyes, and he kept pushing it back. He'd wear a splendid blue blazer, or possibly a fancy uniform, and ask her politely if she could waltz. Of course she could! Gertrudes loved to dance, any step or any tempo. Together they would whirl across the shining floor of the palace ballroom, always in sync, just the two of them, while other couples looked on. But what would she be wearing?

"Wake up, Gertie!" her stepmother shouted. It's one a.m., and time for you to go to work."

"But what would I be wearing?" Gertrudes repeated, still half asleep.

"The same things you always wear, my darling. Blue jeans, a blouse, and sandals."

Gertrudes washed herself, dressed swiftly, and hurried through the dark streets to the old-fashioned dance hall where she was employed, cleaning the bathrooms, sweeping up trash, waxing the wooden floor for tomorrow's customers.

Even at this late hour, there were still a few people dancing near the bandstand: girls she knew and officers from the military base nearby. As Gertrudes watched them, the manager of the dance hall approached her.

"I'm sorry, sir," she stammered. "I know I should be working, not just standing here. I'll stay later to make up for it."

"Relax a moment," the manager replied. "You know, Gertie, I've been thinking about you."

Gertrudes had heard this kind of talk from men before, and she waited silently for the rest of it. But the manager surprised her.

"You're a wonderful dancer," he smiled. "I've seen you waltzing around the floor with a mop in your arms, late at night, when nobody else was watching."

"I'm sorry," Gertrudes said. "It won't happen again."

"Oh, but it should happen," the manager insisted. "Don't you see? We need another girl around here. To dance with customers, I mean. Only to dance with them. Nothing personal, Gertrudes, if you understand me."

Gertrudes agreed to try it. The manager's wife would find her something to wear. And the pay would be twice as much as she was making now. Plus tips! She could buy some new clothes, and a bus ticket to Palm Beach that much sooner.

And dancing! Her thoughts were full of dancing as she did the chores, hour after hour, and trudged home at noon. Too tired to be hungry, she ate some breakfast to please her adoring stepmother. Then she fell asleep and dreamed again of being the princess rescued by an elegant prince.

The next evening, Gertrudes changed into a red satin gown. It barely covered her shoulders, and she was embarrassed. But the manager's wife also gave her a lacy shawl to wear over it. Gertrudes entered the hall more excited than she had been in years.

Night after night, Gertrudes danced with men of every variety, including ranch hands, truck drivers, and military officers. Some of them were good-looking, a few could waltz, yet for her it was just another dance in the arms of a stranger: nothing magical about it. Gertrudes longed to hear the gentle voice of her charming prince, to float around the floor without having her feet stepped on! She was making plenty of money now. As she got closer to leaving her job in Santa Fe, however, the prince's palace in Palm Beach seemed farther and farther away.

Early one Saturday morning, as Gertrudes was getting ready to go home, she noticed a solitary figure at the far end of the hall, dancing with a mop as she used to do. She recognized Fernando, the shy young man who had been hired to take her place cleaning. Tall, black-haired, and barefoot, he moved so gracefully that Gertrudes waited for several minutes before she spoke.

"May I have this dance?"

Fernando looked at her with astonishment, suddenly awakened from his dreams by the voice of a real princess.

Compair Bouki and the Monkeys

Many years ago, when Louisiana still belonged to France, an old man lived by himself among the bayous, those mysterious fingers of water that reach back into the swamps. He liked to eat, and he assured his neighbors that he'd never go hungry; he could catch fish with his bare hands, or find the fruit of mayhaw plants growing wild, or make a tasty drink from the bark of the live oak tree.

But he also said things that made no sense to them; for instance, he claimed that this part of Louisana was actually part of Africa. He also claimed that the trees surrounding his house were full of monkeys. His neighbors had never seen or heard of any monkeys in the bayou country, so they called this old man "Compair Bouki," and told stories about him that were not friendly. "Compair" sounds like a rustic way of saying "fellow" or "man" in French. And "Bouki" is a traditional name in western Africa for the hyena, an animal easily deceived, although it might seem smart enough at first glance.

The story about Compair Bouki and the hungry monkeys amused his neighbors the most. Came the day, they said, when he could find nothing to eat. It didn't occur to him to ask anyone for help. Instead he thought of a plan to get some food his own way. First he gathered wood and built a cooking fire in the yard near his house. When it was hot, he filled his largest pot with water, and put it on to boil. In a few minutes, steam was rising from the pot. Then Compair Bouki marched around his yard, banging on a rusty frying-pan, and shouting:

"Sam-bombel! Sam-bombel tum! Sam-bombel! Sam-bombel dum!"

His words didn't mean anything; he made them up because he wanted to attract the attention of the monkeys. And sure enough, some of the younger ones thought they heard Compair Bouki shouting something about food. They crept closer through the bushes, peeked out, and saw his big cookpot steaming on the fire. Being very hungry themselves, they assumed he had something good to eat. They sang this song:

"Molési cherguinet, chourvan! Chéguillé, chourvan!"

Listening to these monkeys singing, Compair Bouki thought he heard French words for "vegetables" and "stew." He chuckled to himself; the monkeys must be falling for his trick! Five or six of them were looking down from the trees, and he called to them:

"I am going to climb into the pot, and make myself part of the stew. But I don't want to stay there too long. When I say, 'I am cooked,' you must reach in right away and pull me out. Do you agree?"

The young monkeys nodded their heads and gathered around the pot. Compair Bouki jumped in, but the water was boiling hot, so he cried "I am cooked" almost immediately, and the monkeys pulled him out.

Compair Bouki thanked them and said, "Now it's your turn! You climb into the pot, and when you say you are cooked, I will pull you out."

As soon as all six of the small monkeys were in the pot, Compair Bouki put a heavy lid on top, trapping them inside.

"We are cooked! We are cooked!" they cried, but Compair Bouki shouted back at them: "No, not yet! If you were truly cooked, you could not say so."

Compair Bouki went into his house to set the table for lunch. While he was busy inside, three older monkeys came quickly out of the woods, lifted the lid from the pot, and helped their younger relatives to escape.

Not realizing what had happened, Compair Bouki served himself a bowl of hot water from the pot. Believing this to be monkey stew, he found it very tasty! He spooned up more and more until the pot was almost empty, and then he fell asleep. But when he awoke the next morning, he was hungrier than ever, so he decided to play his trick on the monkeys again. As soon as the water was steaming in the pot, he turned towards the trees and shouted:

"Sam-bombel! Sam-bombel tum!

Sam-bombel! Sam-bombel dum!"

A group of eight or nine big monkeys came out of the woods and listened to him.

"When I say, 'I am cooked,' you must reach in right away and pull me out. Do you agree?"

The monkeys nodded. So Compare Bouki climbed into the pot of boiling water, as before, and almost immediately he yelled, "I am cooked!" But this time the monkeys did not pull him out. So he got hotter, hotter and hotter. Finally he was able to cry out again. But it did no good.

"If you were truly cooked," the oldest monkey reminded him, with a knowing smile, "you could not say so."

Quickly the monkeys disappeared among the trees, and there was not a sound to be heard in any direction, except for the clanging, banging noises made by Compair Bouki as he tried desperately to escape from the iron cooking pot.

Then another creature came out of the shadows. This was a striped hyena, a real one, in search of food. It approached the big cooking pot warily, stood up on its hind legs to get a sniff of what was inside, pushing against the edge of the heavy iron lid, but the lid remained in place.

Compair Bouki continued to make banging, clanging noises inside the cooking pot, which convinced the hyena that there must be something to eat. It dropped down to all four legs, circled the pot, noticed how the pot rested on three big stones. Now it got a new idea. Digging with its strong front paws, it undermined one of the three supporting stones, and the cooking pot moved a little. Excited, the hyena dug faster. Soon the pot began to wobble and tilt. Finally it fell over, the hot water poured out, Compair Bouki scrambled to his feet, and the striped hyena hid in the bushes, wondering what might be going to happen next.

Compair Bouki soothed his tender, blistered skin with some salve made from certain plants found in the swamp; then he hurried away to tell the closest neighbors about his clever escape: "I clanged and banged, I banged and clanged, until that old pot could no longer resist my efforts, and out of it I sprang!"

The hungry hyena stayed behind, sniffing and licking the cooking pot as it cooled; but there was no slightest trace of anything resembling food. So the hyena went back into the woods, following the leafy trail used earlier by the monkeys, with a lingering scent in the air that suggested he could catch up with them if he hurried.

CROOK-JAW THE WHALE

In October 1703 the peaceful island of Nantucket, Massachusetts, was struck by a tremendous hurricane, the worst storm anybody could remember. Starting on a Saturday morning, the sky became darker and darker. Trees, sheds, fences were swept away as the wind blew harder and harder. People took shelter in their houses, but soon their yards were filled with blowing sand that piled up against doors and windows. Feeling trapped, some of the younger ones managed to get outside. What they saw was even more frightening than what they had imagined. Huge waves, driven by the wind, were rolling across beaches and fields. Ugly brown foam swirled through the streets of the town. Wooden docks and several small sailing ships had vanished from the harbor. Half the island was already under water, and people feared that they might be swallowed up by the sea.

Sunday morning the wind stopped blowing, and the waves were much smaller. Islanders gathered on a hilltop, discussing what to do. Some thought the storm was over. Others wanted to escape to Cape Cod, on the mainland of Massachusetts, while they had the chance. They approached Nathanael Oakwood, the captain of a merchant ship that was still afloat in the harbor, and begged him to carry them to safety. But Nathanael knew the hurricane was only half over, and he wanted to move his ship far away from land, before it could be destroyed. So he summoned his crew, took his wife and children with him, and quickly put to sea.

Two hours later, as the wind picked up again and the waves grew larger, Nathanael's lookout shouted from the foremast.

"Whale ho!" he cried, pointing straight ahead.

Nathanael couldn't spot it at first, but suddenly his ship rose high on a breaking wave and he saw an enormous whale, pale as death, rising to meet him head-on. Broken harpoons dangled from the whale's gray body, and its great jaws were twisted into a crooked grin.

Although he had no experience dealing with whales, Nathanael was excited by this encounter. He turned the ship's wheel sharply to avoid a collision. The whale turned with him and swam closer. Still not afraid, Nathanael turned further, until his ship headed into the wind, and slowed down. Looking over his shoulder, he saw the whale just behind. Its enormous, crooked jaws were opening, as though to swallow Nathanael's ship in one bite.

"Jump for your lives!" Nathanael shouted.

He quickly lowered one of the ship's boats, and watched his family and crew swim towards it. As soon as they were safe, he spun the ship around again and drove it straight into the open mouth of the oncoming whale, where it stuck like a cork in the mouth of a bottle.

"Try feeding on this, Crook-Jaw!" Nathanael shouted.

He meant to jump to safety then, but the whale's huge jaws closed on the ship's hull with a loud crunch! The whale began chewing on pieces of wood and canvas. When it swallowed, Nathanael felt himself sliding down a long smooth throat, two feet deep in salty water. It was very dark and smelly at first. Then towards the bottom a light appeared, and Nathanael thought he could hear voices.

"I must be dreaming," he said to himself. "Or maybe I'm dead."

He ended up on his feet in the whale's belly: a large, crowded chamber, which was mysteriously illuminated. Among other strange sights, two figures were sitting at a table, playing cards. One was a bony female with glowing red hair, the skull showing through the skin of her scalp. She wore a long white dress made of thousands of tiny shells. The other creature, with horns and a forked tail, appeared to be the Devil.

Afterwards, Nathanael couldn't remember exactly what they had talked about, but the general notion was clear enough: this ugly ruin of a woman wished to marry him, and the wicked Devil would perform the ceremony!

Nathanael refused, of course, and the woman burst into tears. The Devil became very angry. He leaped up from his chair to wrestle with Nathanael. He was very strong, and Nathanael would probably have lost that fight, but then the whale belched violently from eating too much too fast. Nathanael was thrown upward, into the whale's mouth. He squeezed between those terrible jaws, dived into the water, and swam to a floating crate from which he was rescued three days later.

When Nathanael finally got home, and his wife heard this story, she tried to persuade him to retire from the sea.

"There are far too many hazards in whaling, my love," she said.

"But I'm not a whaler," Nathanael protested. "I'm not likely to meet up with that wicked old Crook-Jaw again."

True perhaps. But just to make sure, Nathanael's wife urged him to carry an unusual new harpoon with him on the next voyage: its massive, heavy head was made of solid silver, with a twisted point like a corkscrew, designed to pierce the Devil's hateful heart no matter what clever disguises might be worn.

Daniel Boone Dreams of Chasing a Deer

Daniel "Dan'l" Boone was born in Berks County, Pennsylvania, around 1740. He grew up exceptionally tall and strong, loving the outdoors, hating to be inside, going to school when he had to, fishing in the river and creeks, hunting as often as he could.

Hunting was what he called it, but usually he was just scaring the game. Daniel's father had given him a flintlock musket to learn with, telling him that he had to eat anything he killed. This old weapon was very inaccurate, so Daniel fired harmlessly at rabbits, squirrels, turkeys. He seldom hit what he meant to, but he gradually realized that he was far-sighted. Distant things were extremely sharp and clear to him. Up close, however, things could become blurry and somewhat unreal.

When Daniel was thirteen, his family moved to North Carolina, near the Tennessee border. Daniel took to the deep woods, wearing buckskins and moccasins like an Indian, so that he could run swiftly and silently. He was given a long rifle now, and told it was his duty to put meat on the table. Easy to do! There was so much game that he spent more and more of his time hunting just for the fun of it.

Grizzly bears became his special favorites: big, fast, smart, sometimes dangerous animals. Daniel would roam the Blue Ridge, tracking a brown grizzly mile after mile, until he got close enough to make it turn around and face him. Then, using a knife or just his bare hands, Daniel would growl with joy and fight to the death! Sooner or later, his great strength and his quick reflexes would prevail. To celebrate, he would carve his name on a nearby tree, though he never told his father about it. "Danl Boone kild a bear here."

What else did he hunt? Deer sometimes. They were quite different from bears: fast-moving, but never scary or dangerous. No challenge for Daniel. Usually he hunted them at night with a friend, using the technique known as "shining the eyes." He would run on ahead, carrying a large copper pan of blazing pine knots, into thickets where groups of deer lay hidden. Often a startled animal would leap up, blinded, dazed by the bright light. Then it would stand still, too frightened to run away. Daniel's friend would shoot. Bang! And another deer was ready for the boys to carry home.

Daniel didn't tell his father about this kind of hunting, either, because he felt vaguely that it might be wrong. Yet it was a quick, almost certain way to get plenty of food for his family and any visitors, leaving him free to go after bear or cougar or even a mountain lion once in a while. So he kept on doing this until the night before his eighteenth birthday, when the friend he usually hunted with was sick; Daniel had to get a deer by himself.

Carrying his lighted fire-pan in one hand, Daniel ran easily through the woods, ducking under low branches, ready to shoot if he saw a deer's eyes shining back at him. But he stumbled suddenly on a fallen tree, dropping the fire-pan, which rolled away into the darkness.

As he stooped down to grope for it among the bushes, cussing his far-sighted eyes, the pan seemed to rise up suddenly and come towards him. Daniel couldn't see it clearly. He was surprised, momentarily confused. The bright, glaring light of the fire-pan moved closer. Daniel stood up, forgetting his rifle and backing off. The fire-pan seemed to be following him!

Daniel had a really strange feeling: mindless, stomach-clenching fear, which he had never felt before. He turned and ran, with the fire-pan coming close behind him.

As fast as he went, Daniel couldn't escape from this frightening thing. But then he heard a loud shriek, a clatter as the fire-pan hit the ground. He turned. There with the help of the rising moon, Daniel thought he saw a girl. Dressed in buckskins like himself. White or Indian he couldn't tell. Dark hair down to her waist.

She whispered something, he couldn't understand what, then turned and ran away.

Daniel chased her on and on through the moonlit forest, crossing a high ridgeline after midnight, plunging down into darker valleys on the far side. Running, running, faster and longer than he had ever done before, he felt his lungs about to burst. Ahead he could hear the girl gasping for breath, but there were clouds across the moon so he could no longer see her.

Finally they came to a long field of corn, with several log cabins beyond. Out in the open, Daniel could see better. What's this? Now the girl seemed to have turned into a deer!

Shots rang out from the cabins. Lights. Daniel stopped. Somehow his body felt different. Puzzled, he looked at himself and thought that maybe he too had become a deer!

He raced back to the shelter of the trees. Rested. Listened. Heard a slight rustling sound just beyond him. Felt a cool snout touch his snout. Knew who it was. Felt his heart surge with deep affection. Knew that he would marry her as soon as she became a girl again. Knew that he would run with her whenever she was a deer.

Breathing more easily now, she turned in the direction of the ridge, and he followed her away from there.

ELFREGO BACA
THE FEARLESS DEPUTY

Back in the days when our "Wild West" truly was kind of wild, the men who served as deputy sheriffs could be tall, short, fat, skinny, young, old, brave, or maybe not so brave. Elfrego Baca, for instance, was young, short, and skinny: nothing much to look at. Elfrego kept his new deputy's badge brightly polished, however, and his Colt .44 revolvers polished as well. He wore two heavy gunbelts of extra ammunition crossed low on his hips, with the fancy leather holsters tied down like a gunfighter's.

But what could you tell from that? Elfrego might have been what he appeared to be: a tough young deputy, a deadly shot, ready to enforce the law no matter what. Or maybe he just wanted people to think so. In fact his real life was not very exciting.

After two years of uneventful service as a sheriff's only deputy, Elfrego had to accept the reality that there was very little crime in the town of Frisco, New Mexico, where he worked. His elderly boss, the sheriff, slept most of the day and visited the town's only saloon at night, making any arrests that were necessary. Elfrego was stuck with the boring jobs, such as guarding the few prisoners and fetching their meals, cleaning out cells, and doing the paperwork because his boss supposedly couldn't read or write.

Late one Saturday afternoon in March of 1884, Elfrego finished writing a report, closed the sheriff's large rolltop desk, and strolled down the main street of the town to see what was happening. Very little, as usual. Passing the saloon where his white-haired boss could be seen enjoying some liquid refreshment,

Elfrego continued along the wooden sidewalk to the livery stable. He told the man who owned it that he would need to hire an extra horse on Monday.

"Where you goin', Deputy?"

"Sheriff's sending me over to Pasiente, to deliver a prisoner for trial next week."

Pasiente, slang for El Paso, was just a few miles away from Frisco, and that was where Federal judges held court for southern New Mexico as well as the northwest corner of Texas. Elfrego's prisoner, a Texan, had been in and out of the Frisco jail a dozen times before.

"What's he done this time?" asked the stable owner. "Mean, drunk and disorderly again?"

"No, worse than that," said Elfrego. "He chased a Hispanic girl into the barrio last night. Hurt her pretty bad. Then he beat up her kid brother, who was trying to stop him."

"Nobody told me," the man said.

Elfrego wasn't surprised. Even in a small town like Frisco, the Mexican neighborhood was like a distinct and separate world that most of the other residents didn't know much about.

Back in the office, with nothing to do, Elfrego looked at the latest bunch of WANTED posters. Some mighty bad characters, and some mighty big rewards being offered, but nothing connected with the town of Frisco. Just to keep his mind sharp, though, Elfrego made a list of names, and tried to memorize the faces that went with them.

"Hey, jailer," a voice growled from the row of cells behind him. Elfrego turned. It was the trouble-loving Texan that he had to take to El Paso next week.

"So you're awake," Elfrego responded. "What can I do for you?"

"Steak, fried eggs, and plenty of coffee," said the cowboy, whose name was Frank Magee. "And be darn quick about it! I'm hungry enough to eat the front half of a steer, horns and all."

"I'll bring you some food as soon as the sheriff gets back," said Elfrego.

Magee started cursing. Elfrego ignored him. He had no other prisoners to guard tonight, but now that this troublesome fellow was up and about, he didn't want to leave him alone, even in a locked jail.

"You can't keep me here like this," Magee growled. "I'm an American citizen, first class, and I know my rights."

"You'll appear before the judge in El Paso on Monday or Tuesday," Elfrego replied. "Until then you're staying right here. . . ."

"When I get my hands on you," Magee was roaring, "I'll. . . ."

"Partly for your own protection," Elfrego continued. "A few people in this town would like to have words with you."

"People, did you say, or Mexicans?" Magee sneered. "There's a mighty big difference where I come from."

"But maybe not such a very big difference where you're going," Elfrego said under his breath.

"What's that?" cried Magee, rattling the barred door of his cell. "Why you ornery little. . . ."

At this moment the fat old sheriff walked in, caught the tone of this conversation, burped a couple of times, and sat down at his desk.

"Go get some food for the prisoner," he told Elfrego, tossing him a silver dollar.

"And don't forget my coffee," Magee shouted after him.

Outside, Elfrego breathed deeply and leaned against the wall of the jail for a moment. It would be wrong to hit a prisoner, of course, but he had been tempted! He took another deep breath and looked around.

Sunset had streaked the western sky bloody red between adobe buildings. Though Frisco didn't have much to offer, it seemed a lot better than nothing on a Saturday night. The main street was busy now, with townspeople and cowboys from the nearby ranches, out looking for some kind of fun. As he walked towards the saloon to get a tray of food for the prisoner, Elfrego recognized most of the faces he saw. No, here were some strangers hitching their horses to the post in front of the bank, which was closed and dark. Ten or twelve of them. Dressed like ordinary cowboys. Texans, by the way they talked.

One of the strangers pulled a shotgun out of a saddlebag, and Elfrego instantly reached for his pistols; but a moment later the man put the weapon away, and crossed the street to the saloon with his companions. Elfrego relaxed, followed the strangers inside, and observed them from a distance as he waited for his take-out order to be filled. Everything was peaceful so far. Don't look for trouble, Elfrego told himself.

He bought a Mexican beer, Dos Equis, his favorite brand, and paid for it with small change. Sipping it slowly, he counted a dozen of those Texans, mostly taller than average, each wearing one or two gunbelts like his. They were talking loud and drinking fast. Apparently they had money. . . .

One of them turned towards Elfrego. This man looked like Frank Magee! Maybe a brother or a cousin of the prisoner. Maybe the Texans were going to try a jailbreak! Elfrego picked up the food he'd ordered, and hurried out into the dark street.

He found the sheriff asleep sitting up. Magee, the prisoner, was lying on his bunk with a hat over his eyes. Elfrego unlocked the cell with his right hand while holding the tray of food with his left. When the cell door was wide open, Magee leaped up, grabbed Elfrego around the neck, overpowered him, and snatched one of his pistols, firing a wild shot into the floor. This awakened the sheriff, who reached under his coat for a gun as Magee fired again and killed him.

"Put your other pistol on the table there," Magee yelled at Elfrego, "or you're a dead man."

The young deputy did as he was told. Then Magee leaned forward to pick up his pistol, and Elfrego hit him smack in the face with a full pot of hot coffee. Magee fell to his knees, screaming. Elfrego took both guns away from him, and put steel handcuffs on his wrists, but Magee was too heavy to drag back into a cell. So the deputy used another pair of cuffs to fasten the prisoner's right arm to the heavy iron safe in which evidence was sometimes kept. Magee, moaning with pain, asked for some water. Elfrego pushed a bucket towards him with the handle of a broom.

"Use what's left in that," said Elfrego. Now his heart was beating rapidly like an Apache drum, but he knew what he had to do: lock the door of the jail, secure the windows, and start loading bullets into the Winchester rifles that the sheriff had stored in a closet.

"You're wasting your time, little man," Magee snarled. "The whole front of this jail is going to blow wide open, just about an hour from now. And as for you, chiquito, you're going right ahead to meet your Maker, maybe five minutes after that!"

Elfrego didn't answer. He used wooden tables and chairs to barricade the windows and the door as best he could, and placed the loaded rifles where he could reach them in a hurry. Meanwhile, Magee was crouching behind the iron safe, as close to the floor as possible.

BAM! The front door of the jail, and part of the walll, exploded into chunks of wood and metal. Elfrego felt something cut his cheek. Smoke filled the room. Bullets flew through the shattered window and the gaping doorway. Masked men could be seen dimly in the street, guns blazing.

"Now what, little fellow?" Magee sneered.

"Now I'm going to chase your friends away," Elfrego assured him.

"Fat chance!"

Firing through two broken windows, Elfrego cleared the street with rapid fire from two Winchester rifles, one after the other. Men cried out and scattered. Then he stood in the doorway of the jail with a third rifle, picking off the outlaws as they showed themselves to shoot at him. Gradually their guns were silenced.

Elfrego knew he had been nicked a couple of times, but not seriously hurt. After it was all over, he stepped outside, looked around, and said a brief prayer of thanks. The fierce gun battle had lasted only a short while, maybe twenty minutes at the most, yet the youthful deputy felt that it had changed the direction of his life in some important way.

Years later, while he was studying in Los Angeles to become a lawyer, Elfrego was asked about his famous gunfight back in Frisco, New Mexico. This eager man actually wanted his autograph!

"I heard it was maybe twenty or thirty to one against you," the man said. "I heard you killed more than half of them Texas cowboys before the rest of them gave up."

"Well, there weren't more than twelve to start with," Elfrego replied, "and I'd say I wounded three or four, maybe five, but I didn't kill anybody. I never wanted to kill anybody. To tell you the truth, I really wasn't that good of a shot, and my hand would usually shake when I pulled the trigger. But you know how Texans love to enlarge a story."

☆

ELIZA CROSSING THE ICE

Eliza Harris, the daughter and granddaughter of slaves, lived on a tobacco plantation near Elizabethtown, Kentucky, in the 1840s.

Eliza's granny used to tell her that the town was named after her, but as Eliza grew older and learned more about life, she realized that nothing was likely to be named after her, not even her own children, unless she herself could somehow make it happen! As a teenager, working in the fields from sunup to sundown, she had plenty of time to think. At age eighteen, when she discovered that she was going to have a baby, Eliza decided her child must not be born into slavery; she would run away some dark night soon.

On her first attempt at running away, Eliza got more than a mile from the plantation before one of the white overseers tracked her down on horseback. The dogs cornered her against a thicket of hawthorns, and just slobbered on her bare legs, because they had been trained not to bite.

The overseer said nothing to Eliza. He quickly threw a burlap sack over her head, tied it with twine, and trotted her back to the slave cabins like a turkey on a leash. Eliza wasn't hurt physically, but she ached with anger and humiliation.

After two more attempts to escape under cover of darkness, Eliza was brought before the chief overseer, a burly red-haired man who had no time for either sympathy or cruelty. The plantation was simply a business to him, no different from a factory or a mill, and he was determined to do a good job of running it for his absentee masters.

"You might lose your baby if you run away again," he told her matter-of-factly. "I'm going to have you locked up at night."

Eliza remained silent. Several other slaves who worked the fields were locked in chains each night because they had tried to escape. Eliza learned from their experiences.

"By day those overseers be so busy bossin' everyone," an older woman advised her. "Best you try then."

Younger runaways gave Eliza similar advice, though most were discouraged about trying again themselves.

"Don't know where to go if I do get loose," a man said. "Nobody around these parts goin' to help."

Eliza made one more attempt to escape before her baby was due. She crept to the edge of the field where she was harvesting tobacco and slipped into the woods when nobody seemed to be looking. But which way should she go? Her body felt so heavy and awkward, Eliza had all she could do to walk slowly in a more or less straight line through the trees. Twice she stopped to catch her breath. If she could find a creek and follow it, the hounds might lose her trail. . . .

Beyond the sheltering woods, she climbed a split-rail fence and started across an open field of long grass, with cows grazing in the distance. But moments later, she heard horses galloping. Getting closer. Two of the plantation's overseers caught up with her, one on each side, and held her between them with ropes. Eliza fell to the ground, moaning. When they pulled her upright again, she burst into tears.

"Spare my baby," she begged, before she fainted.

Late that night Eliza regained consciousness, chained to an iron bed, in great pain. She tossed and turned. Someone wiped her hot forehead with a damp cloth. Women's voices gently comforted her. Pain came and went. She drifted off again. The next morning, she awoke to greet her own child: a girl, healthy and hungry and loud.

"What you goin' to name her?" a woman asked.

"Freedom!" cried Eliza, still excited and confused about what was going on. Later the chief overseer told her this name was not acceptable, so she chose Frieda as a substitute, or rather she pretended to. But in Eliza's own mind and heart, her little daughter's name had been Freedom from that very first moment of maternal pride.

With her baby to nurse, in addition to working all day in the fields, Eliza had little time to think about escaping. Eventually the overseers relaxed their vigilance and allowed her to sleep in her own bed, without chains. As the months passed, however, her daughter Freedom was growing bigger and stronger and more intelligent. Again Eliza began to wonder how she could make the dream of freedom come true for both of them.

When little Freedom was almost two years old, several of the male slaves tried to escape together. They stole a wagon and traveled as fast as they could down the rutted country roads that led to Louisville. From there they hoped to find their way to any of the Northern states where slavery had been abolished. But having no clear plans and no help, they were soon caught and loaded into that same wagon, tied hand and foot. Back at the plantation, they were whipped, then chained to posts in the yard.

A white-haired slave named Israel, who knew much of the Bible by heart, tried to comfort these miserable men spiritually. And listening to him speak, Eliza too breathed easier. Yet the peace that she felt did not last very long. Self-assurance swept through her like the heat of righteousness. It wasn't wrong to seek freedom, again and again; it was something she ought to do, she would continue to do!

Eliza kept on asking questions, piecing together her knowledge of her surroundings. The plantation was about twenty miles south of Kentucky's border with Ohio, a state that no longer permitted slavery. But there were obstacles along the way, including other plantations with overseers and hounds. Thick woods and hills, some of them cut by gullies and creeks, separated these properties from one another. Finally there was the Ohio River, deep and very swift, where several runaways were known to have drowned. The shortest route to the river, folks said, was to follow Otter Creek due north, as it flowed through the woods between farms. However, this escape route had been tried so many times that the overseers always looked there first.

"Best try a different way," a friend suggested.

And how to get across the river when she reached it? That was another big problem, to be sure, but Eliza wasn't going to hold back. She'd find a boat, she'd swim, she would do whatever she had to do.

Then someone said the river might freeze, come January or February. This had happened two years before, and several folks had escaped to Ohio across the ice! Eliza felt hope rising strongly within her.

"This time we're going to make it," she assured young Freedom, who smiled up at her trustingly.

November, December, Christmas. . . Eliza waited impatiently for the coldest weather. Most slaves were kept indoors, busy with tasks such as repairing tools and making burlap sacks for the next season, but a few of the men rode wagons to Louisville with the overseers, and loaded bundles of cured tobacco leaves onto flatboats at the river's edge.

"River frozen yet?" Eliza would ask them, when they returned at the end of the day.

"No, not yet."

"Not yet."

"Frozen a little bit."

"A little bit more."

On the first day of February, just before work stopped for the noon meal, Eliza hid Freedom under her long gray cloak and walked out of the barn. Passing the main house unchallenged, she entered the woods beyond it, not heading north towards Otter Creek but west instead.

"Here we go, Freedom," she whispered.

Carrying her daughter, Eliza walked two or three miles until she came to a different creek, frozen solid in some places. There she turned north, using the shadows of trees to guide her, as she had been taught by one of the other slaves. Stumbling, plunging through the thin ice sometimes, Eliza wearily followed the winding creek more than thirty miles, stopping only to care for her sleepy little girl. Hour after hour, day and night, she felt no weariness, no hunger, no cold. In fact the weather seemed surprisingly warm.

At sunrise the third day, Eliza came out of the woods on a high bluff. There was the Ohio River below her: frozen at the edges, but moving in the middle, broken up into flat slabs of ice bigger than barn doors, separated by dark channels of water. Could she get across?

"We're not stopping now," Eliza decided.

Hounds howled in the distance. Eliza didn't look back. She held her precious Freedom tight, and slid down the slippery hill to the river's edge. Hounds were howling louder now. Eliza ran out onto the ice, which was able to support her weight at first. Closer to the middle, though, where the frozen surface had broken up into big pieces, she could see that the whole mass was moving slowly downstream. It was frightening, yet beautiful.

Coming to the first narrow gap in the ice, Eliza stepped across to one of the large floating slabs, maybe twenty feet wide. Though it tilted slightly under her, it still felt solid. At the far edge, there was another gap two or three feet wide. Eliza ran, leaped, and made it. She slipped on the next slab, fell, but scrambled up and went on to the next gap. Leaped. Then another gap, wider. Then another.

"We can do it," Eliza thought, holding Freedom high as she ran, and leaped, and ran on. The more she did it, the easier it seemed.

Behind her the plantation overseers were shouting in frustration, but the dogs had given up already, and Eliza continued her crossing with amazing grace.

ENDLESS HERD OF HORSES

In August 1880, a businessman named Angus McDill traveled all the way from Scotland to Wyoming to buy horses that he could later sell at a profit in the British Isles. McDill was smart and careful with money, too sharp to be easily cheated, but he had been warned that some Americans might be even sharper, so he brought with him a keen-eyed little Scottish bookkeeper to count every dollar and every animal. He also brought along a merry-looking bagpiper dressed in a tartan plaid kilt.

His own personal luggage included a heavy leather satchel designed to carry money; and in one of his inner pockets he had a small silver flask, full of very potent Scotch whiskey.

McDill was going to meet a horse-trader by the name of Jake Dorsey, who had advertised that he would sell as many as five hundred horses for $25 a head, the lowest price around.

Before McDill's arrival, Dorsey made plans with his bowlegged horse wrangler, Buck.

"Scotchmen are supposed to be rich," Dorsey explained, "and this here letter says they want to pay cash. So the problem is how to make our small herd of horses look like it's almost endless."

Buck waited. He knew from past experience that Dorsey would come up with a plan. . . .

"I've got it!" Dorsey exclaimed, after a few minutes' thought. "Buck, you know that pint-sized mountain up at the north end of the mesa, with a narrow canyon along side of it? Here's what I want you to do. . . ."

Saturday morning the Scotsmen arrived at the nearest railroad station. Dorsey met them, loaded them into a buckboard wagon and drove twenty miles across the range towards the place he had in mind. Except for a few pieces of tumbleweed blowing in the wind, the vast Wyoming landscape was dry-looking and empty, and it was already getting hot from the relentless sun.

"I dinna see any horses," said Angus McDill.

"The horses are mostly back in the hills, behind that mountain," said Dorsey. "There's water there, and some cover from the sun, and of course the grazing is better."

When they got close to the small mountain, Dorsey drove part way up the crooked canyon beside it, where he could park the wagon on a broad ledge under the shade of pinyon trees.

"We'll set right here," Dorsey said. "My wranglers will send the horses past us, so's you can check 'em over and count 'em to your heart's content."

"Are these horses truly fit, all of them?" McDill asked.

"Why sure, as far as I know," Dorsey replied. "I've owned them for a couple of months now, and I've yet to spot a sickly one. But if you should happen to notice any critters you don't like the looks of, just holler and we'll cut 'em out of the herd."

Time passed slowly. Looking around, McDill noticed a large wooden box in the back of the wagon. It seemed to be full of nothing but rocks and pebbles. He questioned Dorsey about them.

"They're for ballast," Dorsey replied.

"For what?"

"For the ballast, like in a ship, to add extra weight. Otherwise a lightly built wagon like this would bounce too much on rough ground."

McDill, a sensible man, thought this idea was ridiculous, but he said no more about it.

Soon the noise of many thundering hooves came rolling down the narrow canyon, and the leading horses appeared: six or seven prime stallions, followed by several dozens of other stallions and mares in a growing cloud of dust.

It was difficult to see very much, but Angus McDill felt pleased. These horses were big! Quite a lot bigger than the French and Spanish horses he was used to. Buying them here

at $25 each, he could sell them in Scotland or England or any-
where else in Europe for a substantial profit! He tried not to
show his pleasure. Instead he poured out a stiff drink of Scotch
whiskey for Dorsey and a much smaller sip for himself. Then
he told the bagpiper to play a lively Highland tune called
"Horses' Brawl."

Meanwhile the last of them were galloping down the
crooked canyon and out of sight.

"How many is that so far?" McDill asked the bookkeeper.

"Forty-nine" was the reply.

"That's kind of strange," said Dorsey. "We keep 'em separated into batches of exactly fifty, and I was sure I was giving
you an honest count."

Moments later, an old gray horse appeared, walking slowly by himself, looking tired and ready for a rest.

"There you go," said Dorsey. "That one makes it an even
fifty, like I said."

"Nay, but he's not as healthy as the others," McDill objected. "I won't pay you annathin' for that one."

"Then we'll take him away," said Dorsey, "and we'll owe
you one extra horse when we're done counting this afternoon." He fired a shot from his revolver as a signal to Buck,
who was out of sight at the head of the canyon.

Again came the noise of thundering hooves, as horses appeared in a cloud of dust. The bookkeeper counted, the bagpiper played, and Dorsey accepted another wee sip of Scotch
whiskey, which made him feel just a little bit light in the head.
He smiled; his plan was working just as he had hoped.

McDill was smiling too, until his bookkeeper told him the
count for this second batch of horses.

"Forty-nine," the man reported grimly.

"Are ye certain?" McDill demanded. "Go over your tallies
again for me, there's a good man."

While the bookkeeper was checking his numbers, an old
gray horse came walking slowly down the canyon, looking
tired and ready for a rest.

"Why, that's the same poor weary old beast we saw before," said McDill. "I'm nearly certain of it."

"Nope, that's a different one," Dorsey replied. "I could go down and check his brand to make sure, but I tell you what: we won't count that one either. Let's say we'll owe you two extra head of horses when we're done. Is that fair enough?"

McDill agreed. After a short pause, the sound of thundering hooves was heard again, and horses started coming down the canyon at a gallop. When the last of them had gone by, McDill glanced suspiciously at Dorsey.

"This time I counted only forty-eight," the little bookkeeper called out excitedly. "You're short by two!"

"I'd say there was forty-nine again," Dorsey responded. "But I might have missed one because of dust."

Just then an old gray horse came walking slowly down the canyon, looking tired and ready for a rest.

"And what do you tell me this time?" McDill demanded. "Is it the same weary beast again, or no?"

"Can't be," said Dorsey. "That other one is a mile away by now. But I'll check on it. You fellas eat your lunch and get ready for the next batch of horses."

Dorsey walked quickly up the canyon to find Buck and talk urgently to him, before anything else could go wrong. While he was gone, McDill asked for suggestions from the bookkeeper and the piper. It was time to try a new idea.

When Dorsey returned, the piper was playing a different Highland tune, "Robbers of the Glens," and the bookkeeper was sharpening his pencil with a pocketknife.

"Are we ready for the next batch?" said Dorsey.

"Indeed we are," McDill replied. "More than ready."

He poured another wee drink of whiskey for Dorsey, and waited as the sound of thundering horses came down the canyon again. They galloped past in twos and threes and fours. When the last of them had disappeared through the dust, McDill's bookkeeper announced the total.

"Forty-nine."

"Agreed?" McDill asked Dorsey.

"Sure, I guess so," Dorsey responded. "Yeah, agreed."

All that Saturday afternoon they continued to watch horses galloping past them, and the bookkeeper called out the total of each batch: forty-nine, forty-seven, forty-nine, forty-eight, and so on. Never exactly fifty. And the old gray horse was not seen again.

"Buck's doin' a pretty good job," Dorsey thought.

Finally the show ended, and the bookkeeper announced the grand total for all ten batches: four hundred and eighty-seven horses.

"Not the five hundred I came here for, Mr. Dorsey," said McDill.

"No, not quite," Dorsey replied, "but you're always bound to lose a few along the way, what with rustlers and rattlesnakes and such. I'm glad to accept your count, though, Mr. McDill, and the price that I advertised still stands: $25 a head, as is. I got the legal bill of sale right here, ready to fill in and sign."

"And afterwards, where do you go from here?" McDill asked.

"I'm returnin' to the train station, so's I can catch the afternoon express to Tucson. Buck is comin' too. And I'll be happy to give you fellas a ride to town. The wagon goes back to the place I rented it from. But the herd stays here. And you gotta understand that how you handle your horses is gonna be up to you from now on. Okay?"

"Perfectly satisfactory," said McDill. "And please don't worry your head about a few extra horses that might be missing from the herd. Four hundred and eight-seven will be enough for me!"

"And you're gonna pay me cash," Dorsey reminded him. "No checks or money orders or suchlike things."

"Not to worry," McDill responded. "My bookkeeper will count out the money. It's all in Scottish sovereigns, if you don't mind. Solid gold coins that any American bank should be happy to accept."

McDill abruptly turned his leather satchel upside down, and a dazzling shower of gold spilled onto the wooden seat of the wagon. Dorsey's hand tingled when he touched one of the coins. After years of cheating some people, and being cheated by others, this was the real deal!

"Seems okay to me," he said.

"As the money is counted out," McDill continued, "the piper will help you to load the coins back into my satchel, which is yours to keep, of course, since I won't be needing it any more."

"Why, that's mighty nice of you, Mr. McDill," said Dorsey. "I do know gold when I see it, of course, but I never expected to handle so much of the stuff at one time."

The Scotsman and the rancher smiled at each other again, shook hands, filled in the blanks and signed the paper, which said that on this date, Jacob Robert Dorsey had sold to Angus McDill a herd of 487 live horses for the sum of $12,175, payable in Scottish sovereigns.

Still seated in the wagon, Dorsey took each golden coin from McDill's bookkeeper and passed it along to the bagpiper, who was holding the leather satchel open on his lap, near his bagpipes. Dorsey could hear the clinking of coins, and he assumed the gold was dropping down into the open satchel that was now his. But he was tired and hot and a little fuzzy, from drinking so many wee sips of that fine Scotch whiskey, so he did not pay attention as closely as he might have. . . .

When he finally picked up the satchel, however, it certainly seemed to feel heavy enough, and he thought he could hear the clink of gold against gold inside.

Dorsey and Buck then drove the visitors back to town, Dorsey assuring them it would be easy to hire a few temporary hands for rounding up their endless herd of horses the following week. Nobody worked on Sundays, he explained, so they might as well take a day off to relax themselves.

At the railroad station they all shook hands, and said farewell. Far down the track, a distant whistle from the Tucson express could be heard. Then, as the three Scotsmen walked off towards the entrance of their hotel, the piper began to play another tune: something faint, very slow, very dull. It almost sounded as though his leather bagpipes might now be full of something other than warm air.

"That's mighty strange music they're playing," said Buck.

"Well, the Scotch are a mighty strange breed of people," Dorsey replied. "They think they know it all, of course, and sometimes maybe they're right; but this time I'd say we outsmarted 'em."

FRANKIE & JOHNNY

Frances Ernestine Baker, known as Frankie to her friends, was one of those restless young people of color who drifted into St. Louis, Missouri, during the 1890s. St. Louis was turbulent in those days: less violent than such legendary places as Dodge City, Abilene, Deadwood, or Tombstone, but still tough, tricky, and often dangerous.

Frankie learned this the hard way soon after her arrival. Looking for work at a large downtown restaurant, she said something that must have sounded insulting to one of the busy waitresses. Owww! Faster than the eye could follow, a straight razor slashed Frankie's right cheek. With blood running down her pretty brown face, Frankie wasted no time on tears. She found a barbershop nearby, paid the man to patch her up, and bought a folding razor to protect herself.

Although she was intelligent and ambitious, Frankie couldn't get a decent job after that. Restaurants, stores, offices all turned her away because of her ugly scar. She might have worked in a kitchen or a stockroom, out of sight, but she was too proud to hide her face. Instead she made the rounds of the dance halls, the saloons, and finally the many gambling parlors. At the biggest and best of these, she made a strong impression on the fat black man who ran the place.

"I don't know a thing about card games," Frankie admitted.

"This you can learn, honey, this you can learn," he replied. "But you got somethin' else that nobody could teach you: it's called class."

He was right. Even before Frankie became an expert at dealing poker, blackjack, and other games of chance, she began to attract customers with her unusual good looks, her quick and original wit, her confident attitude of being above it all.

"I'm here because I'm having fun," she seemed to say, "not because I have to be."

Sporting men and women, black and white, crowded around Frankie's table to share in the ups and downs of the game, whether they won or lost. "Some of my biggest winners are losers," Frankie would declare, laughing, and the players would laugh with her. They thought they understood what she meant.

What Frankie really meant, though, was that she was getting hooked: not on liquor or drugs or gambling, but on gamblers. She felt herself developing a weakness for men who bet everything they had, or more than they had, and lost it all, then came back the next night or the next week and started all over again. She met a lot of men like that, since there seemed to be a lot of them around, not only in St. Louis but also in New Orleans, Chicago, Denver, Omaha and other cities with plenty of easy money, where fortunes changed hands quite often. Win tonight then lose tomorrow, win the next day, lose the night after that, and so on.

These sporting men, and the women who accompanied them to St. Louis, began to regard Frankie Baker as the queen of their kind.

"See you at Frankie's," they'd say to one another, although she didn't really own the Twelfth Street gambling parlor where she worked, and her name was not painted on the sign over the door. Frankie simply dominated the scene with her skill and humor from the moment that people first walked into the place, and they remembered her after they left. Dressed in expensive new gowns, and wearing costume jewelry too as she became more successful, Frankie was indeed the sporting queen. She had a way of raising her brown eyes from the card table and surveying the whole room with a slow glance; money couldn't buy that regal attitude.

Into Frankie's view one Saturday night swept a man who caught her interest almost immediately. Tall, dark, and wolfishly handsome, the legendary Jean E. Beauregard had arrived from New Orleans earlier that day with easy money in his pocket and a streak of wildness in his heart. He had heard about Frankie's establishment from other gamblers on the steamboat coming up the Mississippi, and he entered the place like a king: brisk, sure of himself, seemingly certain that people would make way before him.

Frankie and Beauregard spotted each other as the other gamblers cleared away from her table. Something powerful like electricity passed between the pair of them. Frankie asked him what he wanted to play, and Beauregard smiled at her wordlessly for a long moment. Frankie, as cool as she usually was, felt the pulse thudding in her chest.

"Poker," he said finally, in a voice like music.

As there were no other players at the moment, Frankie dealt the cards to play against him, one on one. She was ready to match his skill and daring, but the game was not as challenging as she had hoped. Beauregard kept staring at her instead of paying attention to the cards. He bet large sums carelessly, almost as though he had to throw his money away; in less than half an hour his last stack of poker chips was gone. He left Frankie's table a loser that night, but they both knew he had won her heart.

Johnny Beauregard came back two weeks later with his pockets full of money again, wearing the most outrageous clothes that Frankie had ever seen. Long flat-heeled shoes with mirrors set in the toes. Black velvet trousers, vest and hat, Stetson's special "high roller" style. Embroidered shirt with ruby cufflinks, more rubies on finger rings, on his watch chain, his fancy sleeve garters. And a loose silk coat, money-green like Johnny's eyes, which almost concealed the two ivory-handled Derringer pistols he wore holstered under his arms.

"Won my clothes back at that place on Danneel Street," he told Frankie. "Maybe changed my luck."

During the weeks that followed, Johnny won and lost a lot of money at her table, but Frankie hardly noticed. She was madly in love with him, and she couldn't wait until the gambling parlor closed at three or four a.m. Then Johnny would take her out to eat, to go dancing, and kiss her as though he had personally invented romance. If there had been anybody back home for her to write to, or a close friend in New Orleans, Frankie would have shared her good news with them. But she was on her own now, so she had to be content with singing to herself.

Then came a night when Johnny didn't show up at Frankie's, although he had won a big game of poker the night before. Frankie, losing her cool self-assurance for once, asked people if they had seen him; but nobody had.

So she made the rounds as soon as she got out of work. Twelfth Street, Care, Targee, Pine Street. Many a man, and some she knew, but no Johnny Beauregard.

Later, as she was walking home through a residential neighborhood, she heard his laugh and, turning, saw him going into a small, respectable-looking house with another woman. Frankie didn't stop to think. She pushed open the front door behind them, drew her razor, and cut Johnny so badly that he could only whisper to her in anguish.

"My cousin," he said faintly, and Frankie could hear nothing after that, not even the screams of the horrified woman who shrank away from her in the hallway.

Stumbling out, Frankie wandered the streets in search of a policeman to confess her crime. But she never stood trial for killing Johnny Beauregard; it seems that he had been on the wanted list himself for several murders.

Months later she returned to her gambling job, outwardly the same as before, though inwardly a changed woman. She had sworn to give her heart to no man, and she kept her word until August 1899, when Albert Britt appeared beside her table to serve drinks. He was black, slender, plainly dressed, about thirty years old, so shy that he could barely look at Frankie when she spoke to him. Yet when she saw his green eyes, full of fear and wonder, she was reminded of Johnny Beauregard at the moment of death, and her heart beat resoundingly as it had then.

"I'm suppose to collect four dollars for these drinks," Albert stammered. "Don't mean to interrupt."

"No, the drinks are always free at my table," Frankie replied gently. "Don't worry, I'll explain to you later."

Although she was four or five years younger than he was, Frankie felt quite protective towards Albert at first. He seemed so helpless and unsure of himself. The losingest loser she had ever met! And she wanted desperately to shield him from a world whose dangers he barely recognized. So she moved him into her comfortable home, and fed and clothed him lavishly.

"No need for you to work," she assured him. "I've got more than enough for both of us."

Albert enjoyed this life of unaccustomed leisure and luxury for a while. He ate and drank a lot, and put on some weight, but he had nothing else to do all day while Frankie slept, nor most of the night while she dealt cards. So he got bored, and he began cheating on Frankie with one woman after another.

When she found out, Frankie used his own small handgun to shoot him fatally.

"I loved you," Albert gasped. "I was your man."

"But you done me wrong," Frankie responded, watching his frightened eyes close before she was led away.

FUR-BEARING TROUT

A lot of people go looking for gold, and some of them find it, but some others don't; they have to settle for different things, such as the lead that was accidentally discovered among the hills of Colorado in 1877. There a group of would-be gold miners abruptly decided to become miners of lead instead; so they staked the necessary claims, named their new community "The City of Leadville," bought two wagons full of tools, worked hard, and made a decent living for several years.

Lead had all sorts of industrial uses in those early days, including pipes and window-frames and certain kinds of paint, not to mention the bullets that some people liked to fire out of their six-shooters and rifles in large quantities. Therefore the miners were usually able to sell every ounce of ore they could dig from the earth.

Things were going quite well until the lead miners got word that twenty-four young ladies from Chicago were rehearsing to put on a spectacular show of singing, dancing, and acrobatic exercises at a theatre in Denver the following month. *"For Two Days Only,"* the notice said. *"Single Tickets $5.00 Each, Box Seats $10.00 Per Head. Free Admission If Bald!"*

Denver was only ninety miles away, and most of the miners hadn't seen a pretty girl in two or three years, so they decided to close down their mine for a week or so, and have some fun. But to do it properly, they needed some "citified" clothes to dress up in. And free admission if bald; they liked the idea of saving money by getting rid of their hair. But how?

This problem was solved the following day, when a traveling salesman arrived at the mining camp. His wagon was loaded with boxes and trunks. He displayed a full range of gents' finery, ranging from shiny green suits and fancy yellow shoes to red silk neckties and English mustache wax. He also offered a mysterious liquid called "Patented Hair Subtractor" which was guaranteed to make people bald, for two dollars a bottle. None of the miners had ever paid more than a dollar-fifty for anything that came in a bottle, and they were hesitant.

"Sure it's high-priced," the fast-talking salesman agreed. "But look at it this way: here is the only patented product that will take hair off and keep it off, painlessly and permanently. Or else you get every penny of your money back."

Each of the lead miners bought some of this liquid, used it, lost their hair, and rode into Denver a month later, wearing their new clothes. They found half a dozen busy theatres, and quite a few women who might have been experts at song, dance, or even acrobatics, but not the special young ladies they were looking for. Disappointed, they rode all the way back to Leadville in gloomy silence. And their gloom deepened when they found that a safe containing most of the lead mine's profits had been stolen in their absence.

It took the lead miners nearly a year of extra-hard work to earn back the money they had lost as a result of clever deception and downright theft. During this difficult time, they experimented with various ointments and other remedies that promised to restore their hair, but none of those concoctions did any good at all.

Then one of the miners, Marcus Galena, had to travel home to Chicago because his widowed mother was seriously ill. There he happened to hear about a new "scientific" formula that had supposedly grown hair on the head of a bald gorilla at the Lincoln Park Zoo. It was called Hairzup, and it was mighty expensive, twenty-five dollars per gallon.

Now Marcus had no desire to be as hairy as a gorilla. However he asked people if they had heard anything about Hairzup, and he was taken to see an elderly man who happened to live near the zoo. This man had been bald most of his life. Now his hair hung down to his shoulders, and covered his face and hands. So this Hairzup worked, apparently, whatever its ingredients might be.

Marcus assumed that the other miners would be eager to buy some of this product when they heard about it. So he found the warehouse where it was sold, counted out a hundred silver dollars for four gallons, and started the long journey back to Leadville.

After leaving the train in Denver, Marcus rode through the rolling hills with four big glass jugs of Hairzup tied behind his saddle. He was more than halfway to camp when the horse's foot slipped on a crude log bridge crossing the Tarryall River. Two of the jugs got loose and fell, breaking on the rocks below and spilling their contents into the stream. But there were still two gallons left.

"You try it first," the other miners insisted. "If it works for you, maybe we'll use it too."

Marcus followed the printed instructions exactly, putting Hairzup on his bald head every eight hours, and wearing his hat day and night in order to keep the results a secret. The truth is that nothing much happened. But the other miners still avoided him, and he started feeling lonely. So on a bright Saturday morning in May he got dressed up in his shiny green "city" suit and rode off towards Denver to visit a woman with whom he had been exchanging postcards for the past year or more. As he crossed the Tarryall River he looked down, stopped, and got off his horse. The water was full of strange fish. Trout they looked like, sort of, but trout covered with thick black fur. . . .

After staring at these fish for a few moments, Marcus got an idea. No more of this lead mining for him! Instead, he staked his own property claim to 160 acres of land along both sides of the river, put up some tents and one-room cabins among the pine trees, and advertised in the biggest Eastern newspapers.

Fishermen, hunters, and just plain curiosity-seekers came from far and wide to try their luck fishing for "Fur-Bearing

Trout." They caught quite a few of them, year after year, but the furry fish just kept on multiplying, and Marcus Galena just kept on making money. Presently he had a comfortable house built for himself among the bare boulders on nearby Bald Mountain. He persuaded the lady from Denver to marry him and live there, except for occasional trips to New York, San Francisco, and other places where they found exciting ways to spend his fortune.

And Marcus often smiled to himself from then on, pleased as he could be with the various twists and turns of his life, though he never did grow much hair.

GEORGE WASHINGTON AND THE CHERRY TREE

George Washington was born on a small plantation in the English colony of Virginia, not far from the point where the long and unhurried Potomac River, flowing in from the west, finally meets the waters of the Chesapeake Bay. This is called "tidewater" country, because it is close to the tides of the Atlantic Ocean. It is still inhabited mostly by good-hearted people who live on farms, plant crops, catch fish, raise families, mind their own business, and like to use boats and horses when they go to visit friends.

One summer day in 1735, when George was three years old, he and his family came sailing back from just such a friendly visit up the river to find that their modest wooden home had burned to the ground. It was smoking and smouldering as they stood looking. Almost all of their furniture and belongings had been destroyed, and the fire's cause could not be immediately determined. George's mother thought that they should rebuild the house and start over, but his father had other ideas.

After giving some further instructions to the plantation workers who remained behind, he helped his wife and children back into their boat and took them more than a hundred miles up the Potomac to a much larger plantation that he also owned. There a new house was built. Small at first, this house grew larger room by room as Washington's family grew, and it became the mansion we know today as Mount Vernon.

When George was still a little boy, however, that future comfort and elegance could hardly be imagined. Upstairs his new home had only two bedrooms at first: one for parents and the other for children. Downstairs consisted of a big all-purpose room, with no formal dining room or parlor. Sheds behind the house were used for cooking and other necessities. There was not a hint of the white columns, the wide verandah where George and his wife Martha would sit and rock in later years, looking down towards the river and the woods beyond. Instead of roads and parkways, nothing but footpaths and a rough trail meandering through fields and forests in the direction of Alexandria, Virginia, and what is now our capital city of Washington, D.C.

As simple as it was, young George enjoyed his new home a lot more than he had the earlier one. His older brothers went off to school, but he had some visiting cousins to play with, chickens to chase around the farmyard, trees to climb, the river for swimming, fishing, and crabbing. The farm itself had plenty of things to see and do, though George was not yet big enough to help very much. There was also a blacksmith's shop and a wood joinery, where tools and furniture were produced. And sometimes a few toys were made for the younger children, when skilled workers could spare the time. So George played with twelve wooden soldiers, a red wagon that had horses to pull it, and a clever gadget that made a hand-carved monkey leap up and turn somersaults when two long handles were squeezed together.

He was a bright little boy, educated at home by relatives and tutors, and as he got to be five years old, the simple, familiar pleasures of childhood were beginning to bore him. His older brothers were coming and going freely, on horses of their own, while he usually had to stay home. They were allowed to use real tools, knives, even guns, while George had to be content with pieces of wood and make-believe.

After dinner on his fifth birthday, George asked his father, Augustine Washington, for permission to carry a sword. The response was delighted laughter.

"A sword? George, you dearest, most extraordinary fellow, what will you be thinking of next?"

"But I mean to become a soldier one day, Father, and so I must begin preparing myself as soon as possible."

"My darling boy," his father answered kindly, "you are much too young for such things as swords, and I pray you may never have any reason to use one."

"But, Father. . . ."

"No, George, my boy, a sword is out of the question."

A few days later, after George had given up all hope of getting a sword, his father surprised him.

"Perhaps you can amuse yourself with this gift which just arrived, from one of your cousins in England."

Mr. Washington reached into the side pocket of his coat, and presented to George a slender object wrapped in shiny blue paper. Opening it, the boy discovered a folding knife, with one small blade and a smooth bone handle.

"Father, this is exactly what I need!"

"Use it carefully, my dear son."

During the next year, the little knife become young George's sword, his tomahawk, his wood chisel, and many other things in games he played. He would treasure it for the rest of his life, never losing it, but he quickly saw that he couldn't really cut very much with such a small blade. Again he went to Augustine Washington to make a request.

"I need a saw, Father, or an axe, so that I can help the men clearing brush from the new pasture."

"Very well," his father responded, after giving it some thought. "I will consider an axe or a saw for you, George, when you are six years old. But first you must promise me," he continued, as the boy hugged him gratefully, "you must promise that, whatever tool or implement I give you, it will never be used in harmful or destructive ways."

"Of course I promise, Father," said George, his happy thoughts racing ahead. "But must I really wait until my next birthday?"

"I will think about the question, my son, and discuss it thoroughly with your mother," Augustine Washington assured him.

Not long after their conversation, George and his father watched as the blacksmith finished making a sturdy little hatchet. It immediately took the place of his pocketknife in the boy's daily activities. But now there was a difference. Instead of playing, he could help to do some of the actual work of the household, the daily chores, such as chopping thin sticks of pine for kindling wood, or trimming fresh evergreen branches to decorate the dining room.

At Sunday breakfast in that very room, several weeks later, George's father made a stunning announcement. Somebody new had been hired to take over the management of Mount Vernon. Now that the farm was well established and capable of prospering, George and his family would be moving away.

"Hundreds of fruit trees will be planted here, along with corn and hay, and I do expect them to flourish," Mr. Washington explained.

George felt his own little world falling apart. He withdrew silently to a secret place in the woods nearby, and there he wept.

The next day he felt better, and as time passed with no more talk of moving, he began to hope that his father's plans might have changed yet again.

On a crisp morning in March, however, George saw an English ship tied up to the dock in the river below the farm. Men were unloading dozens of young fruit trees, roots wrapped in burlap, and pulling them up the hill in handcarts. During the next two weeks, several of the fields closest to the house were transformed into orchards. Soon the new manager would be arriving to take charge of the farm, and the family would move away from there. Perhaps forever. . . .

George felt depressed, then angry about this disruption of his young life. Not just angry. Furious! As soon as the planting was completed, and the workmen had left, he rushed outdoors to look at the new trees: apple and cherry, peach and pear, plum and something else he didn't recognize. Such little, perfect, innocent trees, brought all the way from England at very great expense. And now George hated them!

Seizing his hatchet, which he wore in a loop of leather hanging from his belt, George ran angrily through the new orchards, sweeping the blade left and right at branches, buds, and blossoms. He left a trail of pink and white petals behind him. But it was not enough just to injure these new enemies. He wanted to destroy them!

Thwack! He started chopping at the trunk of a cherry tree close to the house. Whack! Thwack, thwack! His hatchet cut deeper. Whack, thwack! Chips flew. Soon the cherry tree was leaning over. Thwack, thwack, thwack! Finally with a loud cracking noise and a sigh of branches, the young tree collapsed and fell to the ground.

About to attack another of the cherry trees, George caught himself and stopped, as though his father was there to restrain him. He still felt upset, angry, but now he felt remorse as well. These trees had done him no harm, after all, and he had been taught to respect all living things.

And his father! What would George's father think, when he was told this terrible news?

All afternoon, George waited by the gate for Augustine Washington to come riding home on horseback from Alexandria. Finally, as dusk fell, he saw the beloved figure of his parent approaching.

"Father, Father!" he cried. "The most dreadful thing has happened to one of our new fruit trees, there, by the house!"

Augustine Washington quickly dismounted from his horse. He examined the damage to the cherry tree, then picked up young George in his arms.

"Whoever did this, George?" he asked.

"I did, Father," the boy said, bursting loudly into tears. "I did it, I did it. I cannot lie to you!"

George wanted to explain why he had cut down the tree. He wanted to say how sorry he was, but his father interrupted, and picked him up.

"Later, my dearest boy, later I'll want to know all about it. But right now, George, the important thing, the really important thing, is that you have told me the truth!"

Riding high in his father's arms, young George Washington looked out over the rows and rows of new cherry trees, which were bending towards him now, almost bowing, in the evening breeze from the river. He didn't need to fight them any more. He felt like a conquering hero.

★

GOLLYWHOPPERS' EGGS

In the early days of this country, farmers usually had to grow or make most of what they needed, because there weren't many places to buy things, and they didn't have much money to spend. Often they would depend on peddlers who walked from one farm to the next, carrying heavy packs of useful items for sale, such as pots and pans, buttons, hair ribbons, shoelaces, books, and small tools. Most of those peddlers seemed to be honest, hardworking men who eventually put aside enough money to buy a horse or open their own store; others had to quit peddling and live on what little they had been able to save, because they were worn out.

But one peddler from Rhode Island, a curly-haired, middle-aged man by the name of Wily Swift, thought of a much easier way to make some money for himself. Instead of selling people the things they really needed, at fair prices, he sold them gollywhoppers' eggs for five or six dollars apiece. Of course five dollars was considered a great deal of money in those days, but Wily was a clever salesman. He would talk for a while before he opened up his traveling pack and let people see what a gollywhopper egg looked like. Then he would bring out this brown hairy "egg" about the size of a football.

"Why, that's the ugliest egg I ever did see," a farmer's wife or sister might complain.

"Yes, ma'am," Wily would reply. "But surely you're not going to buy this egg for its looks. Remember what's inside, and what it can do for you."

Woman or man, young or old, Wily Swift would always tell them the following story:

"About ten or fifteen years ago, the captain of a whaling ship from Portsmouth, New Hampshire, discovered gollywhoppers on an uncharted island in the Pacific Ocean. As you probably know, gollywhoppers are huge, wonderful birds with clean white feathers, whiter than snow. They build their nests in palm trees, lay their eggs one by one, and leave them alone. And these eggs take several years to hatch. I happen to own four of them, myself. I can't tell you exactly when this one will hatch, but it surely is worth waiting for! The lucky person who owns a gollywhopper will bless the day they bought it and marvel at the bargain price they paid, for this is truly a remarkable bird."

"What's so remarkable about it?" someone would ask.

"Well, first of all, the gollywhopper usually eats almost nothing. Thus the cost of upkeep is practically zero. Yet this amazing bird can finish more work in one day than your typical hired hand is able to do in one week: for instance, pulling out tree stumps, plowing the ground with its beak, spreading seeds, or harvesting a crop. It can pick fruit or nuts from several trees at once. It can milk your cow, paint your barn, or guard your chickens from weasels and other varmints. In fact, there's just one thing that a healthy gollywhopper can't do, and I want to be totally honest with you about that."

"What can't it do?" someone would say.

"Well, it just can't seem to stop working," Wily Swift would reply. "If you order it to stop, or even ask it nicely, your gollywhopper will get upset and run away. Chances are you'd never see it again. So maybe you should think twice about paying me five dollars for this egg. Five dollars is an awful lot of money."

"No, I don't mind that," the customer would say. "There's always plenty of things to do around here. Even a gollywhopper wouldn't run out of work, it seems to me."

"Well, that's all right then," Wily would continue. "Here's your egg. Just keep it in a nice warm place, wrapped in an old blanket or some straw, until it hatches."

And then the customer, the farmer's wife or sister, or whoever it was, would slowly count out five dollars in small coins, which they had been saving up for a long time. Wily would thank them heartily and leave soon afterwards.

This story repeated itself many times, for five or six years. Wily Swift sold at least a hundred gollywhopper's eggs to people all over New England, before anyone suspected the truth. He made enough money to buy a shiny new buggy and a good bay horse, with some left over to open a savings bank account in Boston.

Then one summer day in 1836, Wily Swift drove up a rutted lane outside the town of Amherst, Massachusetts, to the farm of Mrs. Alice Robinson. She was a widow, a nice-looking woman who had bought an egg from him three years before. Her sister, a sailor's wife, was visiting from New Bedford.

"Has your egg hatched yet?" Wily asked pleasantly. "No? Well, it should be due just about any time now."

Alice smiled politely, and her sister wanted to look at it. So the egg was brought out, in its tidy box full of straw, neatly trimmed with scraps of pink and blue calico.

Alice's sister immediately saw what this so-called "egg" really was, just an ordinary coconut, but she remained silent for the moment, while Alice and Wiley chatted. Then, having thought about it carefully, she invited him to eat supper with them.

"I'd be only too pleased," he replied.

Alice also liked the idea of Wiley staying for supper. She eagerly offered to wash his shirt overnight, and to use a hot pressing iron on his wrinkled coat and trousers as well, since he had told her he was a traveling man with nobody to look after him.

"Why, that's mighty nice of you, Alice," said Wily. "And if I could sleep in your barn tonight, I'd get up and be out of here in the morning before you knew it."

The three of them had a big jolly meal together, with Wily telling funny stories and laughing at his own jokes.

As the clock struck eight p.m., Wily was already beginning to feel a bit sleepy; so he complimented Alice again on her cooking, and said good night. He left his clothes neatly piled outside the barn door. Then he climbed the ladder up to the hayloft, chuckling to himself, and soon fell sound asleep.

A little while later, as Alice was ironing Wily's coat and trousers, her sister explained to her how she had been cheated by this good-looking peddler. At first Alice was upset, of course, and disappointed, but fortunately her sister had a plan for getting even.

Early the next morning, Wily was awakened by loud noises: his horse whinnying, and women screaming. He climbed down the rickety ladder from the hayloft as quickly as he could, but then he remembered that he had no clothes to put on. So he stopped just inside the barn door, stuck his head out, and hollered towards the house.

"What's wrong there?"

"Oh, Mr. Swift," Alice called back to him, "what a miserable night. How did you ever sleep through it all?"

"Sleep through what?" Wily demanded.

"Why, the gollywhopper bird hatched out of its shell around nine p.m., while I was pressing your coat. You never saw such a commotion! Before I could say anything, that gollywhopper had washed all of our supper dishes, plus the silverware, the pots and pans. Then he scrubbed the kitchen floor. And then he went right ahead, laundered and ironed your shirt, and sewed a button on it, almost faster than we could see him move. Then he dusted the house from top to bottom; it was wonderful, just like you promised, the whole place clean in less than an hour! But I forgot your good advice, Mr. Swift: I asked him to stop working, and that was a big mistake! The gollywhopper got so upset! He started crying and carrrying on, like a great big old baby! He rushed out, hitched your horse to that fine new buggy of yours, and drove off down the lane. What a remarkable sight that was! My sister has gone after him in her wagon, trying to catch him."

"What did this gollywhopper look like?" Wily said slowly.

"Why, just exactly like you told me he would look: a really big bird, with a strong beak, feathers all over, white as snow. I wonder where's he gone?"

"I wouldn't know," said Wily, "but I doubt if we'll ever see him again."

"So am I entitled to get my money back from you?" asked Alice. "I mean to say, having the gollywhopper work just once, for a few hours, doesn't seem like it's worth five dollars."

"Money cheerfully refunded," Wily said, not sounding very cheerful. He had kept most of his money hidden in a secret compartment under the seat of his buggy; there was no telling where it might be now. Then he thought of something else.

"What about my clothes?"

"Why, that gollywhopper took them with him, I do believe," said Alice. "And I'm afraid I can't help you. I gave away all of my husband's things, right after he died."

At this point Alice's sister reappeared, walking slowly towards the barn.

"I found both of your shoes, Mr. Swift," she said. "That gollywhopper, that big old crazy bird, must have dropped them in the road. But every stitch of your clothing is gone for good, you poor man. Whatever will you do now?"

"Well, to tell you the truth, I'm close to being flat broke at the moment, and fresh out of bright ideas. All I have left are my shoes, it seems, and possibly my good name."

"You could stay right here, you know, work on this farm for a while," said Alice's sister. "Harvest time next month. Earn a few dollars, pay Alice back, and then be on your way."

"But what will I wear for clothes?" asked Wily. "Burlap sacks from the barn?"

"Why no," said the sister, smiling. "We can do you better than that. Alice and I are both pretty handy with a needle and thread."

So Wily Swift sat in the barn for several hours, hungry and full of vague suspicions, while the two women sewed together some clothes for him. The only material they had to spare was a pair of old sheets from the bottom of the linen chest: enough to make a white shirt, a pair of white trousers, and some underwear.

Just before noon they gave Wily his new clothing and sent him out to earn his keep, picking blackberries on the hillside. At first he couldn't stop eating what he picked, and this didn't surprise the two women. But once he settled down, he seemed to be a fairly good worker. He filled one pail with berries and started on another. Watching him from the back porch, Alice Robinson smiled as she talked contentedly with her sister.

"You know, dressed all in white like that, our Mr. Wily Swift does look kind of like a gollywhopper at a distance."

"Yes, Alice, that's just what I was thinking," her sister replied. "What I was thinking exactly."

GROUNDHOG SEES HIS SHADOW

Michael Cornelius joined the Navy in May 1928, just a few days after his eighteenth birthday, because he was eager to see the world. He completed basic training at Great Lakes, Illinois, and specialized in weather forecasting. Mike was then ready for action, but it was peacetime; his ship never sailed to Pearl Harbor, Hawaii, or any of the other faraway places he had imagined. So instead of re-enlisting at the end of four years, he quit the Navy, took his saved-up pay and went home to Punxsutawney, a friendly little town about halfway down the road from Pittsburgh, Pennsylvania, to nowhere in particular.

Arriving there on a sparkling October day, Mike was shocked to find several stores out of business, streets deserted, "For Sale" signs on houses. Mike's father, who owned and edited the town's weekly newspaper, looked tired and discouraged as they sat in the office.

"What's happening, Dad?" Mike asked.

"You've been away from civilian life too long," his father replied. "We're having what they call an 'Economic Depression.' That means twenty percent unemployment, closer to thirty percent out here in the boondocks. And things are getting worse instead of better."

Mike wanted to ask some questions, but the look on his father's face told him it was time to shut up. So he left the newspaper office and walked along Punxsutawney's main street.

People passed him with their heads down. Almost nobody seemed to recognize him. By the time he reached the end of the paved sidewalk and started back, Mike was feeling depressed himself.

"I can't stand much more of this," he thought. "I've got to try to do something about it."

After supper, Mike talked with his father again. Then he thought for a while.

"This town needs a gimmick," he suggested.

"A what?" his father asked.

"A gimmick, something unusual, something unique, to make us stand out. One of my shipmates used to talk about gimmicks all the time. He's from Brooklyn."

"How about a baseball team, like the Dodgers?" said his father.

"What a gimmick that would be!" Mike agreed.

They both laughed, and kicked around some other possibilities, but nothing seemed to strike the right spark.

"Punxsutawney has only one gimmick I can think of," Mike's father said finally, "the worst winters in all of Pennsylvania. See what you can do with that."

The next morning, Mike walked two miles out of town to visit with his best friend, Bud Binder, who had taken up dairy farming right after high school.

"How bad have the winters been lately?" Mike asked.

"Well, last year the snow was higher than the top of our barn door for two months," Bud said. "I had to dig a tunnel from the house to feed my cows. The only critter that seemed the least bit pleased about the weather was the old groundhog."

"Which old groundhog?"

"The one that lives up there on the hill. He don't care how deep the snow gets. He just digs his way out and dances around like a kid at a birthday party."

"Show me," said Mike.

He followed Bud to the hilltop, where a dead elm tree stood by itself. Bud pointed to the deep hole between its roots.

"That's where he lives, but you won't see him until the weather is real bad."

After that the two friends talked of other things, and Mike probably made his four years in the Navy sound more interesting than they actually had been. Bud forgot all about the old groundhog that lived on the hill above his farm.

But Mike didn't forget. He went back to look at the groundhog's hole again in late December, when it had been snowing steadily all day. He waited patiently. Just before dark he heard sounds of digging. Then a head appeared, covered with spiky brown fur. Gleaming eyes scanned the hilltop, noticed Mike, ignored him. Teeth showed in a grin. Mike retreated to the edge of the hill, watching as the old groundhog emerged from his hole, stretched and yawned, and did a little dance. Snow was still falling thick and wet, but Mike felt happy for the first time in months.

By February 2, the snow was six feet deep, a record already, and it was still coming down. Mike's father printed a front-page story complete with several photographs of the dancing groundhog. This caused a big stir in Punxsutawney and far beyond. The town's excited mayor visited the newspaper office right away, hoping for a miracle that might somehow bring their depressed little community back to life.

Mike's father was busy, answering phone calls from all over the country, but he put the phone down out of respect for his guest.

"Let me get the story straight," said the mayor, "because I'm going to be talking about it on the radio tomorrow morning. If our groundhog *doesn't* see his shadow, this means we'll have six more weeks of winter, am I right?"

"No, Mayor, it's the other way around," Mike's father explained. "If he *does* see his shadow, we'll have six more weeks of winter."

The mayor had to let this notion sink in.

"O.K., I think I've got it now," he said at last. "But is this something really important, that could make Punxsutawney famous? Is it some kind of a scientific breakthrough, in your opinion?"

"No sir, I'm afraid not," Mike's father replied, with a chuckle. "It's really just some kind of a gimmick."

HARDWAY BILL DOES IT THE HARD WAY

Although he grew up on a Florida citrus plantation surrounded by wealth, Jefferson Davis Milton quit school in 1877, when he was fifteen, to work in a local feed store. A year later he left home for good, taking only his favorite horse, his Sharps rifle, a few old clothes.

Jeff's father, who had little time to spare for such things, decided to send a man after him. Not to bring Jeff back, which might only make the situation worse, but simply to keep an eye on the lad. For this task, Mr. Milton selected a private detective, William Hardaway, who was called "Hardway Bill" because he seldom did things the easy way unless he had to.

Hardway Bill sent telegrams out in all directions: to railroad stations, big-city police, and army posts. He soon picked up Jeff Milton's trail in the Florida panhandle, packed a suitcase, leapfrogged ahead of him by train, and sat waiting in a light wagon as the young man crossed the Pearl River into Louisiana.

Never one to beat around the bush, Hardway Bill introduced himself politely to Jeff, and explained what he was doing there.

"And where might you be heading now?" he inquired.

"South Texas, to stay with my uncle," Jeff replied. "Are you planning to follow me the whole way?"

"I reckon that's what your father hired me for," said Hardway Bill. He paused for a moment, and studied the resentful face of young Jeff.

"But I tell you what," Bill continued. "There is no need to spoil your fun. You ride on ahead, and I'll come along behind you, out of sight. It will look like you're traveling on your own."

That's how they started out, but the arrangement seemed a bit foolish to both of them after a while, so Jeff ended up riding in the wagon with Hardway Bill, while Jeff's horse trotted along behind them.

It took four weeks to find the uncle's ranch, all the way down on the Rio Grande near Laredo, and by then they were easy companions, if not exactly friends.

Jeff spent the next two years punching cattle and herding wild horses, while Hardway Bill kept him company, still acting under orders from Mr. Milton.

When he reached the age of eighteen, Jeff thought he should be on his own at last, but Hardway Bill was stubborn, and Jeff's father was still willing to pay him.

A few weeks later, Jeff got a bright idea.

"Bill, I'm going to join the Texas Rangers," he announced. "See if you can follow me then."

"Now that's a mighty tough outfit," Hardway Bill responded. "I doubt if they would let you in. And besides, you got to be twenty-one to join up."

Hardway Bill knew this because he too had been thinking about joining up with the Rangers, if and when his job as paid watchdog came to an end; but he figured that Jeff would find out for himself soon enough. Jeff fooled Bill, however, by growing a thin mustache and adding about three years to the age he stated on his application. So they signed him up, and Jeff went off to the Ranger headquarters at Hackberry Springs in July, 1880, for training. Hardway Bill did not go along.

Despite the exhausting schedule and the intense heat of a Texas summer, Jeff took to the Ranger's life very easily. He loved every minute of the training program. He learned to shoot better, to ride a little faster, to think for himself in any situation, and above all, to uphold the law. He completed the program with top marks in record time.

At first he was assigned to a company of twenty more experienced Rangers, patrolling the dangerous new towns that were springing up across the Texas plains as two railroad lines were being built. Jeff did so well that he was soon promoted and sent alone to one of those towns. It seems the newly-elected sheriff had telegraphed the Rangers asking for help with a noisy riot of construction workers. They hadn't been paid for weeks, and they were starting to make trouble.

When Jeff stepped down from the train, the inexperienced sheriff was astonished.

"There's only one of you?" he asked.

"There's only one riot, isn't there?" Jeff replied.

He unloaded his horse from a boxcar, rode slowly through the angry mob, and arrested several troublemakers without firing a shot. The rest of the workers went quietly back to their camp, and that was the end of it.

Jeff got his next assignment by telegraph from Rangers headquarters. Seems that a masked bandit, driving a wagon, had held up the bank in Laredo and was last seen racing north. Jeff changed horses twice, intercepted the bandit on a bumpy road leading to San Antonio, forced him to stop, and found that it was his old watchdog, Hardway Bill.

"Why?" he asked bluntly.

"Well, you see, Jeff, after your father finally quit paying my salary last month, I ran out of money, and. . . ."

"For Pete's sake, Bill, you could have borrowed some from me."

"I knew I could," said Hardway Bill with the saddest smile. "I knew I could, Jeff, but that would have been too easy."

The Headless Horseman

Katrina Van Tassel sat at her fancy dressing table one evening, admiring herself in the gold-framed mirror before going downstairs to dinner. This was her birthday, in the year 1840, and Katrina was now twenty years old: tall and graceful and beautiful, with long blonde braids and the bluest of blue eyes. And her new dress was patterned silk, the best that money could buy, blue to match her eyes.

Behind Katrina on the stenciled walls of her elegant bedroom were miniature portraits of notable relatives: some who had died long ago in Europe, others who had come from the Netherlands to "New Amsterdam," as New York was once known, to settle on several thousand acres in the Hudson River Valley, and to develop this fertile land into bountiful farms.

Katrina had never gone to school or college, but she had been well educated by some carefully chosen governesses and tutors, and she happened to be extremely intelligent. She spent hours each day reading the available newspapers and the latest books, so she could discuss any reasonably interesting subject more thoroughly than most of the people she encountered at social gatherings, although she realized this was not the "lady-like" thing for a young woman to do. At home, with her easy-going brothers Hans and Mies, Katrina tried not to show them up too often. But she was sorely tempted when they said something stupid or uninformed!

One young man, Willlem Van Dusen, seemed a little brighter than the others. Willem, or "Vim" as her brothers called him, was the best-looking, too, although a young man's looks were of absolutely no importance to Katrina. She was pleased to find that he had read some of her favorite books, including poetry, and he even had a thought or two of his own about agriculture or politics or the future of the country, although he didn't want to talk about such things with her.

"Let's not go into that now," Vim would say to Katrina, with a twinkle in his deep green eyes. "Let's talk about you."

"What about me?" she would reply, although she soon learned what sort of answers she could expect: "Your beauty, of course," or "Your charm," or sometimes "The way you look when you're happy."

Katrina liked her own appearance very much, but she got tired of talking about herself this way. She would try to change the subject, or else she would find a polite excuse for turning her attention away from Mr. Vim Van Dusen, attractive though he might be. Yet the other young men of her acquaintance were even worse!

"If I had two wishes, and ony two," Katrina said to herself in the mirror, "first I would be rid of this annoying freckle near the tip of my nose; and second, I would find someone truly interesting to talk to."

Katrina didn't get her wish about the freckle on her nose. It stayed with her all the rest of her days, although it faded a little when she was older. But she did get her other wish, in a totally unexpected way. It happened that a new schoolmaster was recruited for their village, a promising young man from the Bronx. He promptly came to call on Katrina's father, who had put up most of the money to hire him.

Katrina overheard part of their conversation from the hall, and she was truly amazed. Why, this newcomer could talk about anything: mathematics, geography, poetry, even the prices of corn and wheat! And her father obviously liked him; she could tell from the roars of laughter as the two of them talked.

Walking out into the large and splendid garden, Katrina imagined that her hero had come at last to rescue her from boredom. She pictured him as tall, good-looking, perhaps even taller and better-looking than Vim, but far too interested in things of the mind to care about his looks! Katrina was sure that he would need a haircut, and his clothes would be those of a Bohemian, an artist or a poet, old and wrinkled and dusty. Nothing serious that couldn't be fixed. . . .

However, the young fellow who came outside later to introduce himself to her was no romantic hero. Tall, yes. Needing a haircut and a complete spring cleaning, yes. But as far from handsome as any man could get: he looked like an overgrown chicken, with a small head perched on top of a clumsy body, and a big Adam's apple that bobbed up and down as he spoke.

"How d'you do, Miss Van Tassel," he blurted out in a strangled voice. "My name is Ichabod Crane. . . ."

Katrina couldn't remember what he said after that, or how she might have responded to him. All she could think of was his incredible ugliness, his physical awkwardness; he stumbled repeatedly as he walked beside her in the garden. But after the schoolmaster departed, Katrina thought about him further, and began to criticize herself. What did it matter if Ichabod Crane was somewhat ugly or clumsy? She was tired of being courted by fine-featured, richly-dressed, graceful young men who usually failed to interest her. At least the new schoolmaster wasn't boring!

The next time Ichabod came to visit, Katrina ignored his looks and tried to pay close attention to what he said. He seemed to know something about everything, and when he got going, the words poured out of him in a rapid, twisting stream. So he talked, Katrina listened, and occasionally she asked questions.

"But why do the planets revolve around the sun?" she might say. And Ichabod would tell her the answer.

Or "How does a river like the Hudson manage to make such a deep valley?" And he would explain it to her.

Ichabod Crane came to visit more and more often. He would look at Katrina intently while they conversed. His ugly face lit up whenever she smiled at him. And sometimes when he departed from the Van Tassels' home he would take with him a tulip or a rose that Katrina had picked in the garden, or a bit of paper on which she had scribbled a few words.

Katrina herself was too busy, talking and thinking about really important matters, to notice such little things. But other people did notice them, including her two brothers and their friend Vim Van Dusen. Hans and Mies thought it was amusing for Katrina to be so deeply interested in nothing but words, words, words. Mr. Van Dusen, however, was not amused.

"That scarecrow!" he muttered to himself. "That poor excuse for a man! He has no right to be making goo-goo eyes at my Katrina!"

Yes, Vim Van Dusen was jealous. But he was smart enough to conceal his jealousy from everyone, especially from Ichabod Crane. Instead he pretended to like the young teacher, who had almost no other friends. He loaned Ichabod an old brown horse, and made sure that he could ride it. And he took Ichabod fishing with him. As they fished, he told Ichabod stories about ghosts and witches and other strange creatures that lived in the woods and came out at night, especially "Bram Bones," the headless horseman. Vim described this fearsome apparition in gory detail: the neck cut clean across by the stroke of a saber, the head dripping blood.

"But that's scientifically impossible, Vim!" cried Ichabod. "A living person cannot ride a horse if he has no head!"

"I'm telling you, Ichabod, I've seen Bram Bones with my own eyes," Vim replied. "He rides this river road by the light of the full moon, and he carries his dripping bloody head tucked underneath his arm."

"Impossible," Ichabod insisted. "Scientifically impossible. You must be mistaken, Vim." But he shuddered with fear, and Vim Van Dusen smiled to himself.

A few nights later, when the moon was full, Vim arranged to meet Ichabod at the river to fish for eels. Ichabod Crane, arriving late as usual, tethered his horse and dropped his fishing rod. As he stooped to pick it up, he heard another horse thundering towards him down the road. Around the bend it came galloping, huge and white in the moonlight, its rider wearing an old military costume. And headless! Yes, he was headless, but there, underneath his arm, was something awful. . . a head! Which was dripping!

Ichabod Crane didn't wait for a scientific explanation. He jumped on his own horse and fled. At the schoolhouse he threw his books and other belongings into the gunny sack he used instead of a suitcase. Then he wrote a short letter to the village officials, making up a reason for his unexpected departure.

After that, Ichabod tried to calm down and go to sleep, but every time he dozed off, the most horrible dreams would seize his tortured mind: horses and riders chasing one another, and a big clumsy chicken running around with its head cut off. . . .

In the morning Ichabod rode his old brown horse to Albany, where he could catch the next boat to Manhattan. As soon as it pulled away from the dock, he felt a little better.

Nothing really bad had happened to him, after all. . . .

He looked back at the peaceful houses, beyond them the sunlit fields of prosperous Dutch farms, and realized he should have left a note for Katrina.

"Oh, well," he thought. "Perhaps I shall get in touch later."

But he never did write to her, for some reason, and Katrina gradually forgot about Ichabod Crane. She was spending more and more time in the pleasing company of Vim Van Dusen. He could talk thoughtfully about some of her favorite books, as they walked or rode horses or danced together, and he seemed to have an idea or two of his own. All he needed, Katrina realized, was an understanding woman to draw him out.

Honest Abe Lincoln

When he was twenty-three years old, Abraham Lincoln decided to run for an open seat in the state legislature of Illinois. He didn't look like a politician: he was homely, uncomfortably tall, badly dressed, awkward as a giraffe on the move. And his previous experience didn't add up to very much: farming, odd jobs, and one year's service as a village postmaster. But he had managed to educate himself pretty well by reading books and asking questions, and he sincerely wanted to serve the people of his district. He knew a lot of them already. Now he was going to talk with others, walking along back roads from one farm to the next.

Early one evening in September, Lincoln stopped near a split-rail fence to wipe his sweaty face and rest for a moment. In the field beyond, a farmer was cutting hay in tidy rows the old-fashioned way, swinging a long-handled blade called a scythe. As Lincoln watched, the man finished another row and then came towards him, carrying the scythe. He was a healthy-looking fellow about the same age as Lincoln, and he seemed friendly enough.

"Looking for somebody?" he asked. "I'm Frank Chapin."

Lincoln introduced himself, and Frank smiled.

"I've heard about you, of course," he said. "And I like what I hear. Some people are starting to call you 'Honest Abe.' But why in the world would a truly honest man want to be involved in politics?"

Lincoln laughed too. "Frank, let me set out my reasons for wanting to be in politics," he replied.

Before Lincoln could explain what he hoped to accomplish, he was interrupted by the sound of a bell ringing at the farmhouse on the hill.

"That's my wife calling me to supper," said Frank. "Why don't you come along, Abe, and eat with us? I'd like to hear more about your plans."

Lincoln hesitated, but he knew that a good meal awaited him at home, so he courteously refused.

"I'll tell you what, though, Frank," he added. "If you leave me the scythe while you're eating, I'll cut a couple of rows of hay for you."

"Why, thank you, Abe."

Frank handed him the scythe, together with the whetstone that was used to sharpen it every so often, and hurried up the hill. At the supper table he told his wife, Peggy, about meeting Abraham Lincoln.

"Sounds too good to be true," she commented.

When Frank returned to the field, he found three rows of hay all neatly cut, but where was the whetstone? Frank couldn't find it anywhere.

"Why in the world would an honest man want to steal a thing like that?" he asked his wife.

"I'm not surprised," Peggy replied. "I told you nobody could be as honest as they say he is."

"It's only worth half a dollar," Frank said. But he felt disappointed. This wasn't just a matter of money.

Thirty years later, when Abe Lincoln was serving as President of the United States, the Chapins visited Washington in order to attend a White House reception with other voters from Illinois. There were city people and lawyers and farmers and small-town folks and soldiers, standing patiently in line to meet the President. Frank and Peggy didn't expect more than a handshake and a brief word or two; but as they approached Lincoln he smiled warmly and greeted Frank by name.

"You actually remember my husband after all these years?" Peggy asked.

"Indeed I do," the President replied, and he described their earlier meeting in some detail.

"That's amazing!" Frank said. "But I have to ask you one

question, Mr. President. Why in the world did you take my whetstone?"

Lincoln thought for a moment, then his homely face lighted up.

"I remember now," he said. "I left your scythe leaning against a gatepost, and I put the whetstone up on top."

When the Chapins got back to their farm, they stopped at the front gate, and Frank stood up in the wagon so that he could see the top of the seven-foot post.

"It's here," he told Peggy.

"I'm not the least bit surprised," said she. "Nobody as honest as Abraham Lincoln would lie about a thing like that."

JESSE JAMES OUTSMARTED

One of the exceptional things about Jesse James, the fast-moving man who robbed so many banks and trains during the 1870s, was that he usually didn't know what to do with his share of the money. He bought good horses for himself and kept a few dollars to live on, but he gave a lot away. "Easy come, easy go," Jesse used to say.

It surely was easy to get money, as the James gang became widely known and feared in Missouri, Kansas, Arkansas, and beyond. And it was easy to get rid of the money, too, when Jesse began helping those in need. Widows and orphans, for instance. And small farmers down on their luck. And army veterans who couldn't find work. To most of them, Jesse James seemed more like a hero than a thief; they wouldn't listen to anything said against him.

Out of all those people, Jesse never forgot a woman he met in October 1871, just after he and his brother Frank held up the railroad freight office in Fayetteville, Arkansas. The James boys got away with nearly five hundred dollars in paper money and coins. As they were riding out of town, with nobody pursuing them, Jesse remarked that it would be nice to stop and have a hot meal somewhere. Frank agreed. They swung away from the main road, onto an inviting trail that led back among the low green hills, and soon they came to a tidy-looking farm with smoke rising from the chimney of the house.

Jesse knocked. Presently a woman came to answer the door, holding a handkerchief to her face.

"What is it?"

The brothers introduced themselves. As Jesse hastily explained that they just wanted a home-cooked meal, and they would pay her well for it, Frank James studied the woman carefully. Tall, slender, wearing a shapeless black dress. Dark hair with streaks of gray. She didn't seem all that old, but her cheeks were wet as though she had been crying.

"Is something the matter, Ma'am?" Frank asked.

"My husband was killed in the war. I haven't been able to collect the money he had coming. Now it's just me and my two children, Stevie and Sue. . . they're at the school down the road. . . I've managed to keep this farm going, but now I've fallen behind with the mortgage payments. So the banker is coming out here at three o'clock this afternoon, and I haven't got enough to pay what I owe!"

She started to weep again, while the James brothers shifted their feet uncomfortably.

"Ma'am, how much do you owe the bank?" Jesse asked.

"All told? Four hundred dollars would do it. I could pay off that mortgage and burn it in the stove, once and for all. But I haven't got but fifty-two dollars saved up."

Jesse had more than enough money with him, so he offered to lend the widow the full amount she needed.

"And don't you worry about paying me right away," he added. "I'll come back this way next year, maybe, and that'll be soon enough."

After hearing Jesse's words, the widow perked up quite a bit. She fixed them a hearty lunch of corn bread and hot pea soup with plenty of ham scraps. It felt good to relax for a while, and they were in no hurry to leave. No hurry at all.

"Nothin' beats home cooking," Frank remarked.

"You can say that again," Jesse replied.

As she poured him a second cup of strong hot coffee, the widow's hand accidentally brushed his arm. Jesse was briefly struck by the thought that a man could do a lot worse for himself than this. But soon his restless spirit took over again; he got up from the table abruptly.

While Frank saddled their horses, Jesse insisted on paying the widow ten dollars for their meal, in addition to the loan of four hundred dollars, and the widow accepted. She stood in the doorway as they left, smiling through her tears.

Shortly after three o'clock that afternoon, Jesse and Frank took the dark-suited banker by surprise as he rode along the trail coming from the widow's farmhouse. The brothers had a simple plan: to rob him of the four hundred dollars they had loaned the widow to pay off her mortgage. That way, they figured, she would own her farm free and clear, so she wouldn't have to repay them anything, and they would be getting their money back to spend or to give away again.

The banker climbed slowly down off of his horse. Sure enough, there was a flat briefcase strapped behind the saddle, but it was empty.

"Where's your money?" Jesse demanded.

The banker twitched his thin black mustache.

"I just spent my money buying a farm back there. If you'll allow me to reach into my coat pocket, I'll show you the deed for the property."

"You mean there wasn't any mortgage on the place?" Frank blurted out.

"None that I'm aware of," the banker replied.

When Jesse and Frank got back to the farmhouse, it was deserted. The kitchen floor had been neatly swept, the dishes were drying beside the sink, and there was a piece of paper on the table, weighted down by one silver dollar.

"Received of Jesse James," the paper said, "Four Hundred & Nine Dollars & No Sense. Signed, Mary Witter. Let this be a lesson to you."

Jesse couldn't see exactly what the lesson was supposed to be, but he thought about that woman for years afterwards, until he got too busy doing other things.

JOE BRODIE JUMPS OFF THE BROOKLYN BRIDGE

Joseph Brodie graduated from high school with all A's and B's in June 1885, but couldn't find a decent job. For six months he washed dishes at a busy restaurant on Broadway while he looked around. Then he began working at a broken-down building called The Museum of Many Wonders, near the Manhattan end of the Brooklyn Bridge. Feeling ridiculous in a purple-and-white plaid suit, his hair slicked down with smelly grease, Joe stood outside and tried to persuade people to go inside, reciting a list of the rare things they would see "for one thin dime, the tenth part of a dollar." Dinosaur bones and unicorn horns, genuine pieces of Abraham Lincoln's own log cabin, a bald eagle's feathers, some ribbons from Queen Victoria's wedding dress; the list went on and on.

Many of these wonders existed only in the mind of Joe's greedy boss, Mr. DeBung. The "Museum" was really just a dark warehouse filled with old junk, but his customers wouldn't know that until it was too late. If they came out and demanded their ten cents back, DeBung pointed out to them the very small sign that said "ABSOLUTELY NO REFUNDS" near the entrance. Even though a dime was worth considerably more in those days than it is now, most people didn't bother to argue. They just shrugged and walked away.

Joe hated this job, yet he kept asking himself, what else could he do? Times were plenty tough, and he needed money to help support a sick father, his mother and three young sisters. So he worked there day after day, repeating DeBung's list of "wonders" over and over again, until he didn't have to think about what he was telling people.

His thoughts drifted off in more pleasant directions: doing something important, becoming famous and rich, getting married to the girl of his dreams. He didn't yet know who this girl might be, but he could picture her as he stood there on the sidewalk all day long. She'd have black hair piled up on top of her head, sparkling blue or green eyes, a special smile just for him, and she'd be smart as a whip! Yes, indeed. With a smart wife to steer him, there was no telling where a promising young fellow like Joe Brodie might go!

July 4, 1886, was the hottest day Joe could remember. He was sweating inside his heavy plaid suit. There were very few customers for the Museum, as most people stayed home or went to Coney Island for a swim. The hours dragged by. Joe tried to persuade Mr. DeBung to close the Museum early, but it was no use. DeBung wanted every last dime he could squeeze out of the unsuspecting public.

"You're not tough enough for show business," he sneered at Steve. "If the weather's too hot for you, why don't you go and take a flying leap from the Brooklyn Bridge? That should cool you off!"

"Oh yeah?" Joe muttered, under his breath. "You just wait. I'll show you who's tough."

Joe left the Museum after work, and walked swiftly through the sweltering streets to the Brooklyn Bridge. It soared above him, with steel cables and beams shimmering in the heat. He rushed up the walkway to the bridge's highest point, and looked down at the swirling currents of the East River. Such a long way to jump!

"I can't do it," he had to admit to himself. But he didn't want to give old DeBung the satisfaction of knowing this, so he made his way to the muddy edge of the river, plunged in, and splashed around for a few moments. The cold, slimy water felt just wonderful! Then he hurried back to the Museum, his suit dripping, and caught DeBung by surprise.

"I did it, you see? Don't tell me who's tough!"

DeBung didn't believe him at first, but Joe kept insisting.

So the scheming DeBung came up with a new pitch. Steve still wore his plaid suit, but he sprayed himself with a water hose before greeting people each day. DeBung introduced him as "the only man who ever jumped off the Brooklyn Bridge and lived to tell about it."

Joe lived with this lie for more than two weeks. The tabloid newspapers picked it up, and a lot of people came to The Museum of Many Wonders because they wanted to meet him.

He was going strong until July 23, when he was approached by a brisk young woman with black hair piled high on top of her head, the most sparkling green eyes, and a smile that thrilled him through and through. Introducing himself to her was no problem; she already knew who he was!

"I've been assigned to write a story about you for *Harper's Weekly*," she said. "Will you tell me exactly what happened?"

Joe Brodie looked at her intently, and saw in her expression the lifelong promise he had been searching for.

"Yes, of course I'll tell you," he replied, "but there's something else I've got to do first. It will only take a few minutes. Do you promise to wait for me right here?"

— ✳ —

JOHNNY APPLESEED

Stories about Johnny Appleseed are as plentiful and scattered as the apple trees he planted when Ohio was still a lightly settled Territory at the edge of the new American frontier. For instance, the Amariah Watson family used to talk about an odd-looking man who approached their isolated farm one summer day in 1812. He walked right into the kitchen without knocking, and scared young Mrs. Watson half to death. Seating himself at the table where she had been rolling out dough for bread, he blessed her, told her to fear no evil, then tried to explain why he was wearing only one shoe.

"You see, ma'am," he began, holding out his other foot, which was bare and swollen, "this foot has been guilty of offense in treading most unmercifully upon one of God's creatures. . . a rattlesnake, to be exact. . . and as a punishment, I am exposing it to the harsh surfaces of the roads I walk."

His gentle smile reassured her, in spite of his shaggy-looking hair and his ragged, mismatched clothes. He carried an old Bible in his hand and a big leather sack over his shoulder, but no weapons.

As the man went on speaking, Mrs. Watson gradually realized who he was: Johnny Appleseed, though she had never actually seen him before. People described him as a harmless drifter who appeared in Ohio once in a while, from somewhere else. And they called him "Appleseed" because he planted seeds to grow apples on parcels of unclaimed land, then traded them or sold them or simply gave them away to folks more needy than himself.

Johnny Appleseed left the Watson place soon, having refused any morsel of food or drink, but Mrs. Watson saw him fold a handful of seeds into the soft earth of her barnyard before he vanished down the lane. Years later she could never bake an apple pie without recalling him.

Many other Ohio families were glad of Johnny Appleseed's visits, because he usually left things better than he found them. And people added to his legend as they told one another bits and pieces of what he had been saying and doing. Such as:

Buying a sick cow or hog, and nursing it back to health.

Entertaining children with songs, and comforting the elderly.

Shouting Biblical verses into the echoing wilderness.

Enduring cold and pain as though he couldn't feel them.

Making peace with unfriendly Indians.

And always planting some apple seeds, here, there, and everywhere, from the sacks that he carried in a canoe or packed on a borrowed horse or on his own back.

But nobody seemed to know who Johnny Appleseed really was, where he came from, or why he chose the forests and hills of central Ohio to be his promised land.

The real name of this puzzling man was Jonathan Chapman, and it turns out that he had no roots in the Midwest. He was probably born in Massachusetts sometime in 1774 or 1775, on the eve of the American Revolution. His parents were poor but devoutly religious people who believed in sharing whatever they had with others, for the love of God. So they died penniless when Johnny was still just a young boy, and left him with nothing. Before long he disappeared into the growing stream of orphans and abandoned children who wandered around the country during those years of uncertainty and conflict: frightened, homeless, often starving children. Some were taken in by other families, and cared for, but many were left to fend for themselves.

Johnny survived the miserable hardships of his childhood in New England, and lived to be seventy-two years old; but he never outgrew the habits of a hungry, homeless child. He ate things that other people threw away or fed to animals. Reluctant to live indoors, he slept in haystacks and caves, in barns and livestock pens, in hollow trees or holes in the ground, seldom the same place more than once or twice, until he gradually began to trust people.

His strange clothing and footwear were rags and castoffs, but these he changed often as they were given to others in need. His funny-looking metal "hat" was the pan he used for cooking. Later, because strong sunlight hurt his eyes, he fashioned a wide sombrero from scraps of paper and wood.

Encouraged by voices only he could hear, Johnny made his way southward through New York and New Jersey while still in his teens. He worked for food at some of the big farms around Lancaster, Pennsylvania. He also learned to read there, and when he left, the children's teacher gave him four or five old schoolbooks as well as a large Bible. He refused to part with that Bible until the day he died. But he soon figured out a way to share his other books, tearing them into sections of ten to twenty pages, then offering them to people he met as he went along. If these torn-out pages made no sense to them, if they couldn't read at all, it didn't really matter much to Johnny Appleseed. All that really mattered was the sharing.

Now he walked westward, following the wagon tracks of pioneer families who were heading for the Ohio frontier. Somewhere beyond the fruitful village of Orchard Hills, Pennsylvania, he found a lame horse that had been left to die beside the trail. Johnny wrapped its sore leg in some of his own rags, and led it across a valley, through sweet-smelling apple trees, towards the distant lights of a farmhouse. The weary horse fell asleep standing up, leaning against a tree, and Johnny did likewise to keep him company. The next morning the farmer agreed to care for Johnny's horse in exchange for work, picking apples ten hours a day until the trees were bare.

Johnny was allowed to eat apples freely as he worked, and he was pleased that his horse enjoyed them too. The red, delicious fruit seemed like food from Heaven. And after the harvest, he learned, thousands of apples could be squeezed in a big wooden thing called a "cider press" to produce the most refreshing drink. Even more interesting was the fact that heaps of apple seeds accumulated in the bottom of the press, and the farmer usually threw most of them away.

Johnny continued working there, making cider, until his horse was well enough to move on. Before leaving, he asked permission to take a sack full of apple seeds with him.

"Why?" the farmer asked.

Johnny Appleseed just smiled, because he didn't know how to answer such a question. But as he rode away the following day, holding the rope he used for reins in one hand and his Bible in the other, he seemed to hear voices telling him where to go next, and what to do. It didn't occur to him that he would encounter any difficulty in getting there.

Two days later he came to the Allegheny River, which had risen so high from autumn rains that his horse couldn't cross it. Nearby several families of Indians had camped. So Johnny courteously offered them apple seeds, which they courteously declined, but with gestures they did express an interest in his horse. He was usually generous to others, of course, but he hesitated, because he had become fond of the animal. Yet these Indians might need it more than he did.

Trade canoe for horse, they suggested. Still he felt hesitant. Trade two canoes? Yes, he nodded, I will do that.

So Johhny Appleseed gave the horse a farewell pat and glided down the river with two canoes, towing one and paddling the other as the Indians had taught him. The wide river became so rough, however, that the canoes almost capsized. Then it occurred to Johnny to lash them together, side by side, like a double-hulled boat. That is how he and his sack of apple seeds survived the rapids where the Allegheny meets the Monongahela to form the Ohio River. And that is how he traveled when he left the Ohio, many miles further downstream, to follow a network of creeks northward into the land of his legend. Again and again he visited that region, bearing his gifts of seeds, flowers, songs, prayers. And sometimes other things.

Barefoot and limping, Johnny Appleseed came out of the

woods on a bleak winter day near Isaac Madden's tumbledown cabin. Madden, an unsuccessful farmer who had tried to borrow money from everybody for miles around, was reading the Bible to his hungry family of five.

"Give us this day our daily bread," he prayed.

Johnny Appleseed, entering uninvited, heard those familiar words with a joyful heart.

"And forgive us our debts, as we forgive our debtors," he rejoined.

Isaac Madden jumped up from his bench, surprised, but the three children were very glad to see this visitor.

"It's Johnny Applesauce!" a little girl shouted gleefully. "Do you have a present for me?"

Johnny Appleseed almost always had something he could give away to children, but this time his pockets were nearly empty. Reaching deep, he found a short length of pink ribbon, which he cut in two so that the little girl could share it with her older sister. For the boy, however, he could find nothing special, so he emptied out his leather sack and offered his last handful of apple seeds.

"Plant a tree," he suggested.

"The tree of life," the boy replied.

"That's it," Johnny agreed ecstatically. "The tree of life."

Judge Roy Bean and His Pet Bear

In the 1890s a short, nervous-looking Texan named Henry "Hank" Ketchum decided to try his hand at cattle rustling. He had been fairly honest up to that point, working at a general store in Del Rio, but the struggling store went out of business and Hank couldn't find another job, so he thought he would just steal a few head of cattle and sell them for whatever price he could get. Then maybe he'd use that money to move to Oklahoma and start over.

Hank saddled his broken-down horse one evening, and rode out across the prairie to the nearest ranch, figuring that the wealthy owners would never miss a little livestock on a moonless night. He swung his rope overhead, around and around in a big loop, as he had seen cowboys do in rodeos, and then flung it in the general direction of the nearest steer. Or what might have looked like a steer in the dark. Actually it was a sleepy horse belonging to the ranch foreman, who happened to be sitting on it at the time, taking his turn at guarding the herd. Hank's swirling rope hit the foreman right smack in the face, knocking his hat off and making him see stars for a moment.

"What in tarnation?" the foreman yelled. He raised his shotgun, squinted in Hank's direction, fired a couple of shots, and quickly put an end to Hank's brief career as a cattle rustler. Tied up loosely with his own rope and prodded by the ranch foreman, Hank was forced to walk the two miles back to town, hoping he could find a way out of the trouble he was in.

But the Texas laws about rustling cattle were generally clear and simple in those early days. They were especially clear and simple in that particular part of Texas, where a man known as "Judge" Roy Bean often decided who was guilty of what. Roy Bean was also in business as a saloonkeeper, but he had studied the law for a while, somewhere or other, and he had two thick law books that he used to quote or misquote from. Since there was no other legal authority for many miles around, lots of folks brought their legal issues to him for a decision.

Judge Bean's "courtroom" consisted of the rear area of his saloon, where a thick slab of blackjack oak rested on two empty barrels. He sat behind this "bench" with a glass of bourbon close to his left hand and a Remington .44 army revolver next to his right hand. When Hank Ketchum was brought before him and accused, the Judge had nothing better to do, so he listened attentively to every detail of the case, from both sides, and then made his decision.

"Guilty of cattle rustling as charged," he said. "Mister Ketchum, you are hereby fined five dollars cash for court costs, and sentenced to death by hanging. That's my ruling."

Judge Bean was just about to adjourn the court, when suddenly a better idea occurred to him.

"Hold on a minute," he told his helpers. "Bring the prisoner back here. A plea for clemency has been entered."

Hank stood anxiously before the Judge for a second time, wondering what was going to happen to him next.

"Mr. Ketchum, your sentence is hereby reduced to thirty days of animal husbandry," the Judge declared. Having no gavel, he banged the handle of his pistol down on the wooden slab, and that was that.

"Court adjourned!"

Hank didn't know just who or what clemency might be, and he wasn't sure about animal husbandry, either. However it sounded a whole lot better than being hanged by the neck, so Hank politely thanked the Judge and followed him outdoors.

Behind the saloon a large brown bear lived alone, in what used to be a corral for the Judge's horses. Hank soon understood that he was going to be living there too. The bear came over to the gate, sniffed at Hank, and waited as the Judge locked Hank inside.

"This here is Lily, the light of my life," said the Judge. "Feed her and brush her coat for thirty days, sing her a song now and then, and your thirty days will be done before you can say skid-ee, skid-oo!"

Hank gradually adjusted to his new way of life, eating when Lily ate, sleeping when she slept, and singing her the songs he had learned as a drummer boy in the Army, such as "Yellow Rose of Texas" and "When Johnny Comes Marching Home." The big bear especially liked marching around and around the otherwise empty corral, following Hank as he sang.

After a month of this, Judge Bean was so pleased that he added thirty more days to the sentence, and Hank realized that he might be stuck there forever. The next moonless night, he climbed out of the corral to freedom. Lily followed him, naturally. The two of them walked away unchallenged, disappearing into the dark reaches of the Texas prairie as they headed for the distant hills. Lily found a cave of friendly bears living out there, and went no further, but Hank kept going for several more weeks, following old Indian trails until he stumbled into the unclaimed oil fields of Washington County, Oklahoma, and struck it rich.

KILROY WAS HERE

Near the end of World War II, an American soldier named Jim Donahue came home to South Bend, Indiana. He was so tired he wanted to sleep for a week, but he proudly carried a heavy duffel bag full of souvenirs: helmets, flags, medals, and insignias from four different armies, among other things.

Jim's greatest treasure, carefully packed in a little box, was a smooth piece of dark metal with the words "Kilroy was here" written in chalk. Joe put it on the shelf in the living room, between his bowling trophies, and wouldn't let anyone else touch it.

"What is it?" his children wanted to know.

"Part of a German tank," he told them.

"What does it mean?" his wife asked.

Jim explained how he had found this thing among the wreckage of an Italian village, after a tough battle.

"I was the first GI to enter that town," he said. "At least I thought I was. The whole place was full of smoke, and some of the houses were still on fire. I ran from doorway to doorway, afraid of snipers. But the town was empty. Down the street, I saw this German Tiger tank stuck between two ruined buildings. The hatch on top of the turret was wide open. So I climbed up to have a look. Inside I found 'Kilroy' written on this steel panel next to the radio. I unscrewed it and took it with me."

"But what does it mean?" his wife persisted.

"It means some other GI was the first one into that town. Into that tank. I thought I was, but I wasn't, do you see what I mean? I can't figure out how anybody could have gotten in there ahead of me, but somebody did."

"Maybe some German wrote it. Or some Italian."

"No, this was strictly American. For GIs only. Whoever got anywhere first, got to any hard-to-get-to place, I mean: they would write these words for other guys to find."

"But who was Kilroy?"

"Just a name, I guess," said Jim. "It could just as well be Smith or Jones; or Dwight D. Eisenhower, for that matter."

Many years later, Sergeant James F. Donahue went to a reunion of war veterans in Detroit, and got to talking with some of his old buddies about Kilroy.

"I heard it was all a fake," said one veteran. "There was no such person."

"No," said another. "There was a real guy, but he didn't use his right name."

"Couldn't have been just one guy, or one platoon of guys," said Jim. "They had to of been in too many different places at once."

"So who was Kilroy?"

"I'll tell you," said a quiet man with a scarred face. "I happened to hear the story from a cousin of mine, who grew up near Quincy, Mass."

The other veterans gathered around, and the quiet man continued.

"There really was a guy named Kilroy: actually a civilian, Ralph Kilroy, who worked at the Fore River Shipyard in Quincy during the war, building destroyers. His youngest brother, Paul, a sailor, had been killed on a freighter that was torpedoed by a German U-Boat, out in the North Atlantic. After that, Kilroy did everything he could to get into the war, but he had flat feet and bad eyesight, so they wouldn't take him.

"Then he decided that making ships would be his way of fighting back. And he put his name on each one he worked on. I mean, he couldn't do it officially, or put it where too many people would see it right away. So just before a ship was launched, he would crawl 'way up inside the bow, or maybe climb the mast to the crow's nest, some place like that, and write 'Kilroy was here.' And sooner or later somebody would find it, and the idea would spread."

"I saw it in Korea," a veteran said.

"My nephew saw it in Vietnam," said another.

"So there you are," said Jim. "It wasn't just a guy, it was a whole lot of guys, trying to give everybody a laugh."

"But whatever happened to Ralph Kilroy?" a young veteran asked.

"Why don't you call him up and find out?" one of the others replied. "If he's for real, maybe he's still listed in the telephone directory in Quincy, Mass."

The young veteran went looking for a phone booth. A few minutes later he returned to his expectant friends.

"I got the number, and dialed it, and somebody answered," he reported. "But Kilroy wasn't there."

THE LAST GUNFIGHT OF
BILLY THE KID

William H. Bonney was born in New York City on November 23, 1859. After that, not much is known about Billy's childhood, except that his mother took him to Santa Fe, New Mexico, when he was three, and he killed a man for speaking rudely to her, in Silver City, when he was twelve.

Then he evidently wandered around the West for several years, living and working on cattle ranches, learning a little Spanish, learning things about how to handle people, but above all learning how handy he could be with guns. He had those extremely sharp eyes, fast reflexes, and a cool, heartless attitude towards simple matters of life and death. Thus with almost any kind of a gun, he could hit anything that stood still, and almost anything that was moving: a bear far away, grouse flying up from sagebrush, or those reckless shooters and gunslingers who got in his way and foolishly tried to beat him to the draw.

Shortly before his own death at age twenty-one, Billy used to brag that he had killed twenty-one men: one for each year of his life.

He wounded dozens of others in gunfights, but incredibly he was never hit himself, until Pat Garrett, who was once his close friend and ended up his last enemy, shot him dead.

At that time, Pat had recently been elected Sheriff of Lincoln County, New Mexico. An unlikely lawman, he might have become an outlaw himself if certain things in his life turned out a little differently. He had met Billy the Kid about three years earlier, before he started wearing a badge. They took to each other immediately, although they seemed like exact opposites.

Pat was tall, thin-faced, soft-spoken, originally from Louisiana, a little slower than Billy to draw his gun, and sometimes a lot slower to actually pull the trigger. Billy was just five feet eight inches tall, almost handsome, with a carefree smile and the unreadable eyes of a killer. Strolling past the stores and saloons of some dusty little cattle town, Pat would be gazing at the grassy hills beyond, wondering if he might own a ranch there someday, while young Billy would be staring down each stranger as they approached, hoping that one or another might have enough nerve to start something.

When Billy the Kid was offered money to fight in the cattle wars of Lincoln County, at age eighteen, he urged Pat Garrett to come in with him, but Pat had the good sense to say no. The sharp-eyed leader of Billy's side, L. G. Murphy, was a cattleman whose herds never seemed to get any smaller, no matter how many head of cattle he sold. The leader of the opposing side, John Chisum, owned so many steers that he had never thought of counting them. . . until somebody tipped him off. Now Chisum was accusing Murphy of stealing his cattle in a big way, and Murphy was trying to pay Chisum back quickly and cheaply, with lead instead of gold.

Billy, easily the fastest gun on either side of this feud, killed several of the Chisum cowboys and gradually assumed command of Murphy's gang of gunslingers and thieves. Later, when Chisum brought the law in on his side, Billy shot five members of the posse, including Sheriff Brady, whose job was taken over by Pat Garrett the following year. As more and more men on both sides were killed, news of this cattle war spread across the country, and the President of the United States sent a well-known general to make peace. Murphy and Chisum agreed to stop fighting, but some of Murphy's men did not. Led by Billy the Kid, they holed up at the far end of a remote canyon, and continued to rustle cattle on their own.

Billy had now become a wanted criminal, and the reward offered for his capture, dead or alive, was steadily increasing. Local sheriffs and U.S. marshals went after him with larger and larger posses, yet Billy always managed to avoid their traps or to shoot his way out. He had as many hiding places as a coyote has holes in the ground, and he became so quick and clever in the last year of his life, dodging from one place to another, that some people doubted he would ever get caught.

Finally, near midnight on July 14, 1881, Pat Garrett discovered the entrance to Billy's last hideout, surprised him, and shot him in the dark. Billy died instantly.

Garrett hung up his Sheriff's badge a few months later, and never carried a gun after that. When asked for his thoughts about Billy, he took a piece of brown wrapping paper and composed something like an epitaph to be read at the funeral.

"The Kid had a lurking devil in him. It could be a good-humored, jovial imp, or sometimes a very cruel and bloodthirsty fiend, as circumstances prompted. Lately it seems that circumstances favored the worser angel, and the Kid fell."

MOLLY PITCHER WINS THE DAY

Herman Hays and Mary Ludwig were an odd-looking couple. She was a tall, strong Pennsylvania German woman, comely and sensible, who had turned away one suitor after another before Herman came along. He was short, not much to look at, maybe ten years older than Mary, but sparkling and witty. He amused her the first time they ever met, at her uncle's blacksmith shop in Schwenksville, when he offered to purchase twenty old muskets on account.

"On account of what?" Mary asked.

"On account of General George Washington needs guns to fight the British redcoats, and he has very little money at this moment," Herman replied, with his most winning smile.

"That's not funny," Mary said, but she returned his smile in spite of herself. "Do you work for General Washington?" she continued.

"Not exactly," Herman admitted. "Let's just say I represent his interests, whenever he allows me to do so."

"And he needs these guns my uncle has been fixing up?"

"Precisely," Herman said.

He came back in July with a small amount of cash and a scribbled note supposedly from the General. Mary was skeptical. Her uncle, however, would do anything he could to help "The Father of His Country," as Washington was fondly known among German immigrants in Pennsylvania.

"Let Herman take the muskets," Mary suggested, "but I'll go with him to make sure he delivers them to Washington's army."

It was a long, slow wagon ride through eastern Pennsylvania and across New Jersey to Washington's encampment near Monmouth. To pass the time, Herman told Mary about himself, from his birth in a prison in Liverpool, England, through his service as gunner's mate on a British warship, to his arrival in America, penniless and free, just three years ago. Mary had never heard any story half as exciting.

"And every word of it true, or nearly so," he told her with his charming smile.

"Oh, Herman, you silly man," said Mary. But he delighted her, and truth to tell, she delighted him as well. By the time they reached the Delaware River they were in love, and they stopped briefly at a church in Trenton to get married.

The next day, crossing the sun-baked flatlands of New Jersey, they heard the heavy, thunderous sounds of cannon fire in the distance.

"Three-pounders," said Herman. "That'll be the Hessians, the British mercenaries, blowing holes in our lads from a safe distance."

"Don't the Americans have cannons too?" Mary asked anxiously.

"Not many in this part of the country," Herman replied, "and not much ammunition, so they generally don't fire until the redcoats are almost on top of them."

He urged the weary horses forward, while Mary clung to him. Their wagon moved through the scrub pines into a wide clearing, where American soldiers formed a thin defensive line. Others lay wounded on the ground. Hundreds of British redcoats were advancing towards them.

Then Herman saw some Americans struggling with a cannon they had captured from the British. He quickly hitched his horses to the big gun, swung it around, and showed the untrained young soldiers how to clean it and load the cannonballs weighing three pounds each.

"Ready, Aim, Fire!" Herman shouted. Then they repeated the cleaning and loading, more quickly this time. "Ready, Aim, Fire!"

With Herman in charge, the captured cannon was fired repeatedly and accurately at the approaching British troops.

Meanwhile, Mary found a metal pitcher somewhere and start-ed carrying water from a nearby spring to exhausted soldiers. Then a troop of red-coated cavalry attacked them, swinging sabers and shooting pistols. Mary cried out as Herman fell be-neath their hooves. One by one the Americans were hit. The captured cannon was silent.

"Molly, Molly Pitcher, bring us water," a voice cried weakly, but Mary had no more time to be merciful now. Somehow she managed to load the heavy cannon as she had seen Herman doing it, and fired one shot after another into the midst of the oncoming British soldiers. Some were killed or wounded, others ran away into the woods.

"You have won this day for us, Molly Pitcher," an Ameri-can officer shouted.

But Molly didn't hear him; she thought only of finding poor Herman's body, loading it into the wagon, and driving back to Schwenksville with her grief.

It made her feel just a little better to learn that General Washington had named her "Sergeant Molly" later that day, when he was told what she had done to help America win its war of independence.

—✷—

MORE THAN ONE JOHN HENRY

John H. Davidson lived with his mother, his father, and his grandfather in the peaceful town of Fairmont, Virginia, until the time came for him to go to college at Georgia Tech. He was a handsome, well-built fellow, sometimes seen with a chemistry or physics book in one hand and a tennis racquet in the other, and he seemed destined to do great things. But his life story really began when he was just six years old, coming home from school in tears after his first day in the first grade. His parents were both working. His kindly grandfather, recently retired from a job with the state highway department, sat waiting for him on the shady front porch of their white frame house.

"What's the trouble, John Henry?" his grandfather asked.

"The trouble is my name, Grandpa," the little boy sniffed. "Some of the older kids are making fun of me because I call myself John Henry, like the song."

"But you are John Henry," his grandfather exclaimed. "Same as your daddy and same as me. I was there when they named you."

"Oh, you know what I mean, Grandpa," the boy replied. "I'm not the real John Henry, I'm not big and strong, and the boys are making jokes about me."

"Come sit for a while," said his grandfather. "Tell me what you know about the real John Henry."

"Well, like the song says, John Henry was a steel-driving man. He helped to dig a tunnel through a mountain, for the railroad."

"And what does that mean exactly, a steel-driving man?" his grandfather continued.

"I don't know," the boy admitted.

"Then would you like me to explain it to you?"

"I sure would, Grandpa."

So the grandfather got two glasses of cool buttermilk from the kitchen, and a plate of their favorite blueberry muffins, and they sat on the porch while he told his grandson the tale.

"Well, the real John Henry was a working man, first of all: big and strong, yes, but not the biggest, maybe not even the strongest. Yet he had an unusual amount of pride inside of him. John Henry just couldn't stand to see any man, black or white, work harder or better than he did."

"He was black," the boy said.

"He was black, sure enough, like you and me, but everyone black or white respected him for what he could do. When it came right down to work, pure and simple, the color of a man's skin didn't make a whole lot of difference."

"So what was the steel-driving part?" the boy asked.

"Well, said his grandfather, "just picture what they were trying to do, more than a hundred years ago. Here was this new railroad being built, and here was this mountain. The railroad track couldn't go over the mountain or around the mountain, you see; the track had to go through it. We're talking about a tunnel at least a mile long, maybe more."

"And the whole mountain was solid rock, wasn't it?" said the boy.

"Solid rock, that's right, and in those days there wasn't any of the heavy equipment they use now. So men had to blast their way through that old mountain: blast and then shovel up the pieces of rock, then blast again and shovel again, clearing as little as ten or twenty feet a day. Working from both ends of the tunnel and hoping they would meet in the middle."

"Did John Henry do the blasting?" the boy said.

"No, John Henry made the holes to put the blasting powder in. He had to hit a long steel bar with a sledgehammer, over and over again. Inch by inch that steel was driven deeper into the rock, maybe five or six feet deep for each hole, to make it deep enough. Then other men would put the blasting powder in several of the holes at once, and light the fuses, and run back out of the tunnel, and. . ."

"Wham!" the boy exclaimed.

"Wham is right," his grandfather agreed. "The noise was so loud, you'd think the whole mountain had exploded, and everything was covered with dust. But when they went back in to shovel out the pieces, there usually wasn't all that much to shovel."

"Then John Henry would have to make more holes ?" the boy asked. "Driving the steel again?"

"Exactly right. Other men drove steel too, of course, but John Henry could drive it harder and faster than anybody else, working ten or twelve hours a day."

"Like the song says, Grandpa, he was the best in the land."

"He surely tried to be. John Henry worked so hard he broke some of the company's sledgehammers. He wore out those bars of steel. Bent them or twisted them or snapped off the points. And he wore out some of the men who held them in place for him while he swung the hammer. If John Henry wasn't the best in the land, nobody could tell him the name of any man who was better."

"But then something happened," the boy said.

"That's right. One day John Henry's boss asked him to compete against a steam-drill, a new invention that might someday take the place of men swinging hammers and driving steel."

"Was the steam-drill like an electric drill, that you could hold in your hand?"

"No, this was a big old contraption, with all kinds of pipes and boilers, and a steam-hose attached to a drill so heavy that most men couldn't even pick it up."

"What happened, Grandpa?"

"Well, the men from the steam-drill company heated up about a thousand gallons of water in one of those big iron boilers, to make plenty of steam. As soon as everything was ready, John Henry and the steam-drill man, a white man, shook hands. Then they took their positions in the tunnel facing the rock, about ten feet apart, side by side, ready to start."

"Then what happened?"

"The boss just yelled at them to go, and they surely did! At first the steam-drill was doing better than John Henry. It drilled about four feet deep into the rock, while John Henry hadn't driven his steel but a foot or two. A lot of the men who had bet on him were now wishing they could put their money on the steam-drill instead, but of course it was too late to switch. When John Henry realized that he couldn't catch up, he stopped and asked his boss a favor."

"A favor!" the boy cried. "What kind of favor?"

"John Henry wanted to try using two sledgehammers at once, left hand, right hand, left hand and right, so he could drive the steel rod twice as fast. No man had ever done this before, but his boss said okay, so that's what John Henry did."

"Bam with the left! Then bam with the right!" the boy exclaimed.

"Yes, indeed. And John Henry caught up with that steam-drill, little by little. Then it seemed like the drill was running out of steam. It huffed and puffed, but didn't go nearly as fast as before."

"Then what happened?"

"The drill stopped. So John Henry just stopped and waited while they heated more water to make more steam. Then the drill started up again, and John Henry started too. He went really fast at first. Later on, he began to feel dizzy. He needed water himself, but the steam-drill man wouldn't stop and wait for him to drink it, so John Henry just kept on going. He got so dry he wasn't even sweating any more, though he was working very hard and the day was hot. Some of the men told him to slow down, to quit. Do you know what he did?"

"He just kept going," the boy said, "and he won."

"Yes he did, and the people who owned the steam-drill were so ashamed about losing that they took their equipment back to the factory and tried to improve it."

"What ever happened to that old steam-drill?" the boy wondered.

"I don't rightly know, but I don't believe it was ever used again."

"And what happened to John Henry?" the boy asked. "He died, didn't he?"

"That's true; not right away, but a few hours later, back in the bunkhouse where he had lived with the other men. He died quietly, without saying very much to anybody. Maybe it was a heart attack. There was no doctor there to examine him. But anyway, they gave him as fine a funeral as they could, the following Sunday. People came from all over West Virginia and from other places even farther away, to pay their respects."

"Were you there, Grandpa?"

"No, but my daddy was. His name was Chester Davidson. I was born not long after that, and given the name of John Henry."

"And then my father, and then me," said the boy.

"That's right," his grandfather agreed. "Now let me ask you something: are you going back to school tomorrow and cry about your name?"

"No," the boy said slowly, "I don't think so."

"Well then, what are you going to do?"

"I'm going to do what the real John Henry did. I mean that other John Henry, 'cause I'm a real one too. I'm going to figure out some way that I can be the best in the land."

"That's the idea," his grandfather smiled.

"But you know what, Grandpa? If that old steam-drill runs out of steam the next time, I'm not going go stop and wait for it. I'm going to keep right on driving my steel!"

The Original Ark'n'saw Traveler

Shelby Pendleton moved from Kentucky to Arkansas in 1829 and settled in Chicot County, close to the Mississippi River, as a cotton planter. With his polished Southern manners, soft voice, and refined appearance, young Mr. Pendleton made friends easily among the hospitable families owning large farms near his, and he enjoyed the lively parties and formal dances to which they frequently invited him. It was a rural society, quite limited in some ways to be sure, but surprisingly up-to-date in such things as the latest fashions, music, and financial news, so he seldom regretted the decision to make his home there.

As the years went by, however, Shelby Pendleton became increasingly curious about the remoter parts of Arkansas, the back-country and the Ozark Mountains, where small clusters of poor whites and poor black people were said to live in nearly total isolation from the outside world. He had to see this other "Ark'n'saw" for himself. Therefore he was pleased to join a small number of gentlemen who were traveling on horseback to the farthest corners of the state during the political campaign of 1840, hoping to find support for the re-election of President Martin Van Buren against a strong challenger.

Pendleton became separated from his companions in a heavy rainstorm west of Little Rock, but he decided to press on regardless, in spite of being wet and cold, because the most interesting places lay ahead of him, and his horse was still fairly fresh. At a remote crossroads called "Lost Corner" in the Ozarks, he thought he might dry himself off and stay the night. Perhaps he could even say a few words on behalf of the President.

His audience wasn't very large: just the bearded man sitting on a tree-stump in front of a dilapidated house, a woman banging pots inside, five or six young children peering like possums from the shadows. The man seemed to be busy, tuning his squeaky fiddle, but he looked up as Pendleton approached.

"Hello, my good fellow," Pendleton began.

"Hello yourself," the bearded man replied sourly.

"Sir, can I get to stay the night?" the traveler continued.

"No, Sir, you surely can't git there from here."

"Well, how about something for dinner?"

"Nice of you to offer, Mister, but I just et."

"I'm really hungry, haven't had a bite since early morning; can't you give me anything to eat?"

"Hain't a thing left in the house, not a morsel of meat nor a dust of corn meal."

"Well, how far is it to the next house?"

"Don't rightly know, I never been there."

"So I'll have to stay in your house tonight, won't I?"

"Well, Sir, the roof of my house leaks."

"Why don't you stop it from leaking?"

"It's been rainin' too much."

"Well, why don't you fix the roof in dry weather?"

"It don't leak then."

At this point the bearded man began fiddling a scratchy tune that drew the children out to caper in the yard. Inside the house, the banging of pots had ceased. Whip-poor-wills were calling from the woods across the road.

Shelby Pendleton breathed deeply, rejoicing, looking at the jolly, unspoiled children and the high forest surrounding them: here was the real "Ark'n'saw" he had hoped to find!

When the bearded fiddler stopped playing, Pendleton asked if he could try his hand; he then offered the same tune himself, a little slower but with more precision.

"Well I'll be switched," the bearded man exclaimed, and slapped his thigh loudly. "You never said you war a fiddler, stranger."

"Not as good as you," the traveler assured him. "But now, Sir, how about a night's lodging in the house? Name your price."

"Why not?" said the man. "Give me a two-dollar gold piece and go on inside then, whilst I see to your horse."

Pendleton paid, entered the house and found his way to the kitchen, hoping to be fed. He was surprised when the middle-aged woman looked at him indignantly and refused to let him stay.

"But Madam, I paid your husband quite handsomely to sleep in this house," the tired traveler protested.

"No, Sir, you never did," said the woman.

"But he. . ."

"That man ain't my husband, and this here ain't his house."

"You mean I've been misled?" the traveler gasped.

"I wouldn't know about that," the woman replied. "But you sure as heck been Ozarked."

Paul Bunyan and
His Blue Ox "Babe"

Shortly after graduating from Radcliffe College in June 1920, Winifred Winslow learned that a very distant cousin had died and left her a lumber company near Green Bay, Wisconsin. According to the cousin's Milwaukee lawyer, this totally unexpected bequest included several buildings, a sawmill, an experienced crew of six, and a cardboard box full of unopened mail, which was forwarded to Winifred. Mostly bills, she discovered, but a few checks as well, and a letter offering to purchase the whole business for one hundred thousand dollars.

"Take the money and run," Winifred's father advised, glancing up at her from the newspaper he was reading, the *Boston Evening Transcript*. "Get yourself some new, glamorous clothes, pick a husband, settle down."

Winifred ignored her father's advice, as usual. She filled a large trunk with high-laced boots, shapeless trousers, sensible sweaters, and sturdy cotton underwear and stockings. Then she said good-bye to a sweet young man she had been seeing, and started out on her fateful journey from Massachusetts to the distant wilderness of Wisconsin, changing trains at Chicago and again at Milwaukee.

The lumber camp looked like a disaster area when she arrived: old buildings falling down, sawmill spewing out dust and chips of wood in all directions, logs piled around haphazardly. But Winifred soon found that the lumbermen, lumber "jacks" they called themselves, worked hard and generally knew what they were doing. It remained to be seen if they would take orders from a "mere woman," a citified one and an Easterner at that. She decided to stay on, and give it a try.

When her parents visited Green Bay a year later, Winifred proudly showed them the tidy camp, the new roof on the bunkhouse, the men in their clean outfits coming and going, the neat stacks of freshly-sawn boards and beams. Her father had brought some mail from Boston, including a new offer of two hundred thousand dollars for Winifred's lumber company.

"They're upping the ante," her father commented. "Sell now, and make a tidy profit. Buy a dressmaking business or some such thing, if you like."

Winifred rejected the offer.

Two weeks later, her crew of six expert lumberjacks quit to take higher-paying jobs at another logging camp across the lake. Just as Winifred was thinking about quitting too, a huge bearded man appeared at the doorway of her office, stooping to see inside.

"Name of Paul Bunyan," he said. "Heard you need help, young lady. Tell you what: I'll do the work of fifty lumberjacks for the wages of five."

"Indeed, Mr. Bunyan?" said Winifred, in a voice very much like her father's. "That's quite a tall order. You must not overburden yourself. Suppose we say you'll do the work of ten men to start with, for the wages of two."

"You're asking me to do just a little sliver of what I'm accustomed to, ma'am," said Paul Bunyan. "But I'll see if I can slow down enough to suit you."

Winifred watched him closely at first, but he worked so quickly that she soon gave up. He could chop down thirty good-sized trees in an hour, have them trimmed and stacked next to the sawmill in twenty more minutes, then cut them into twelve-foot lengths, twice the size of fence-posts, faster than her mother's Irish cook could cut up string beans.

"But how can you posssibly move all this wood down to the lake, and make rafts of it?" Winifred asked him.

"No problem," said Paul Bunyan. "Babe will help too, just as soon as she gets back from vacation."

Babe? Winifred waited, expecting to see something like a

large female version of Paul Bunyan himself, muscular and deep-voiced; but Babe turned out to be a gigantic blue ox.

"And she's blue because. . . ?" Winifred asked.

"Babe's blue 'cause she was born in the sky over Lake Michigan," Paul Bunyan replied. "That's where she goes every year on vacation. Up amongst the stars."

"Yes, of course," Winifred said to herself.

Paul Bunyan gathered into one great bundle all the twelve-foot lengths of wood that he had cut, and securely tied it with roots and vines. Then he heaved the entire load onto Babe's broad shoulders, walking behind her as she carried it down towards the lake.

"And what will Babe do now?" Winifred asked.

"She says she wants to try running the sawmill."

Winifred sat alone in her tiny office, while Babe did a day's work in the blink of an eye. Twenty-foot boards flew out of the noisy sawmill like giant bullets coming from a military machine gun. . . .

A week later, feeling strangely discouraged, almost depressed, Winifred sent a long Western Union telegram to her father. She told him that running the lumber camp was getting too easy for her, and he telegraphed his reply at once.

"KNOW WHAT YOU MEAN. SUCCESS COMES TOO QUICKLY TO MOST OF US WINSLOWS. SELL THE COMPANY FOR HALF A MILLION. COME HOME, DAUGHTER. GET INTO SOMETHING MORE CHALLENGING FOR YOURSELF, SUCH AS THE HARVARD SCHOOL OF EDUCATION."

After thinking it all over until the setting sun could no longer be seen through the high pine forest beyond the lumber camp, Winifred Winslow was inclined to follow the advice of her father for once. Becoming a teacher might be just the thing for her!

But Winifred changed her mind before the Fall semester

started. Teaching could wait a while. There was something more important that she wanted to do first. Using some of the money she had received from the sale of her lumber company, she rented a two-room office in downtown Boston and opened the Blue Ox Employment Agency, the first of its kind, helping bright young women to find productive and profitable careers in business.

Pecos Bill Rides a Mountain Lion

Bill Kimble left home at age eighteen, for one reason or another, and made his way to the well-known "Bar None" ranch in West Texas, near the Rio Grande River. He wanted to be a cowboy. He was possessed of enormous strength and determination, although he had no work experience to speak of.

"You can't hardly ride a horse. You've never roped a steer. You don't know one end of a branding iron from the other," said the hard-eyed cattleman who owned this sprawling ranch. "So what use are we supposed to make of you here?"

"I'll try anything," Bill replied. "Just give me a chance."

"Anything?" the rancher said doubtfully. "We'll have to see about that."

In exchange for room and board and a dollar a day in cash wages, Bill took the back-breaking job of hauling water from the Rio Grande to fill some shallow clay basins where thirsty steers could drink. There were dozens of these man-made basins scattered across the huge ranch, and Bill worked really hard from sunup to sundown to keep them full on hot summer days, using leaky wooden buckets. At first he tried to carry two or three full buckets with each hand, but he spilled too much water that way. One morning his boss, the ranch foreman, showed him a broken-down old wagon in the barn.

"You'll have to fix it up and pull it yourself," the boss said. "I've got no horses to spare for things like that."

Bill was somewhat scared of this boss, a mean little fellow who looked like a cactus with a mustache, so he didn't argue. He repaired the wagon with some pieces of wood, and made a harness of ropes to pull it with.

Things went better for a while. From week to week, however, Bill noticed that the level of water in the Rio Grande was lower and lower. It was getting harder and harder for him to fill his buckets, even out in the middle of the river. Finally he had to tell his boss the bad news: there was no more water to be had.

"Well, you'll just have to find water somewhere else," his boss replied, "if you want to keep on working here."

Bill didn't realize his boss might be asking too much of him. He went jogging that night, in a wide circle around the ranch, looking for ponds or streams to keep the cattle supplied with water until this dry spell was over. His search seemed hopeless: now even the smallest water holes were empty. At dawn he scanned the sky, but it was cloudless as usual. There might be no rain until the weather got cooler in the fall.

"What about the Pecos River?" his boss asked.

"Dry as a bone," said Bill.

"I heard there was water in it, further up," the boss insisted. "Go take another look."

Bill hastily finished his breakfast of steak and eggs, and hurried out the door. By noon he had reached the Pecos. He followed the dry, sandy bed of the river northward. After a few more miles he discovered some shallow puddles of water. . . not enough to fill many buckets, but surely better than nothing. . . and a tiny stream trickled down from one puddle to the next. Then some passing cowboys told him there was a lake, a pretty big one, in the hills farther north. Bill hurried back to the ranch and asked his boss if he could borrow a plow.

"For what?" the boss demanded. "You gonna be Farmer Bill now? I thought you was aiming to be a cowboy."

"I'll cut a channel up to that lake," Bill explained, "but first I'll dig out a pond at this end, so the water won't just run away when it gets down here."

Bill took off his shirt and boots, and started pushing the plow around the dry clay soil. He loved to work hard. He kept at it all day, without taking a break, despite the heat. By supper-time, when his boss and the other hands came riding in from the range, the hole for the new pond was half a mile across and forty feet deep.

"Not bad," his boss admitted. "I can see where you're trying to go with this. But it still don't have no water in it."

Early the next morning, Bill made an opening in the north side of his empty pond, and started cutting a channel to the north. He pushed his plow swiftly across miles of empty prairie, then up the dry riverbed of the Pecos towards the lake he'd heard about. Hour after hour, plowing through clay or sand or gravel, Bill kept on going. When he finally got to the lake, however, it was almost empty, and the many hoof-prints of cattle around the edges told him it must be heavily used.

"Got to go further," Bill thought.

As the moon rose he left the lake behind, following the dry riverbed, pushing steadily to the north with his plow. At dawn the next day he crossed into New Mexico, but there still wasn't enough water in the Pecos River to wet more than his bare feet. Somewhere in the hills between Santa Fe and Las Vegas, he found a bubbling spring where the river actually began, and there was nothing more to plow; he couldn't go any further.

That afternoon Bill sat beside his river, watching a shiny trickle of water coming out of the ground. Tired now, and more than a little hungry, he closed his eyes. As he slept the sky slowly darkened, and warm summer rain came pouring down, filling the narrow riverbed, overflowing the banks of the Pecos, soaking the dry land.

Bill woke up, saw what was happening, and laughed happily. At last his job was done!

"But I'm not going back to cattle-ranching in Texas any more," he decided. "No Sirree! I been there, I done that."

Reaching into a nearby cave, Bill pulled out a reluctant rattlesnake, made a loop of it, and roped a wet, bewildered mountain lion to ride on. Snake and lion soon understood who was in charge.

As the rain stopped, Bill dried himself with tumbleweed and moved out, eager for the adventures he knew he would find in the high desert west of the Pecos.

PETTICOAT PIRATES

Mary Adair was a teenaged girl who lived with her grandmother near Cape Hatteras, North Carolina, in the early 1800s. Both of her parents had been drowned years earlier, during a terrible storm, and her grandmother didn't seem to care how Mary spent her days as she got older. . . .

So Mary skipped school whenever she felt like it, and seldom looked at books. She loved to play by herself on the deserted beaches, acting out stories that her daydreaming granny had told her about exciting men and women of long ago.

Sometimes she would run down to the water's edge, then turn around quickly and face the land, as though coming ashore from some imaginary ship.

"I am Don Punky Dillingham," Mary would shout to the sky and the indifferent gulls. "I have come here to discover the fountain of youth!" And she would use the blade of a rusty old shovel to dig in the sand: shallow, watery holes that were washed away by the incoming tide.

Other times, Mary would dress up in a blue cloak and high black boots that had once belonged to her grandfather, and pretend she was conversing with a seagrape bush.

"Sir Waldo Ranleigh at your service, Madame. And you, I presume, are Her Majesty the Queen of Elizabeth City?"

The seagrape didn't respond, of course, but Mary pretended that the mighty Queen was commanding her to sail the seas in search of gold and jewels. She could vaguely picture what such treasures might look like. All she needed was a ship!

Eagerly she searched the horizon day after day. But the few vessels that passed were headed north towards Virginia or south towards Florida; they had no reason to approach the empty Carolina coast where Mary lived.

One hot afternoon, while Mary was dressed up in her cloak and boots, she fell asleep among the seagrape bushes and dreamed that pirates had landed on the beach nearby. At least she thought it was a dream. Men's voices could be heard, and laughter, and sounds of metal clashing against metal. When Mary sat up and peered through the bushes, she saw half a dozen barefoot villains dressed in red-striped jerseys and bell-bottom trousers, with a leader wearing boots and cloak like hers. The leader also wore a long blonde wig and a plumed hat, which Mary wanted for herself. She straightened her costume, took a deep breath, and boldly approached the strangers.

"I am Sir Waldo Ranleigh," she declared. "And now, Captain Fancy, if you please, I will have the very hat off of your head!"

There was a roar of laughter from the pirates, for that is what they were. The leader stepped closer, grasping a cutlass and handing another to Mary.

"Take my hat from me, girl, if you can," she said.

Mary was surprised to hear the voice of a young woman. All at once her imagination deserted her.

"But... but. . . ." she stammered.

"Butting is for goats," the young woman answered, as her crew laughed again. "I am Jacqueline Caldecott, better known as 'Calico Jack,' the terror of the seas. If you won't fight me for my hat, I've got no use for you."

Still not sure if she might be dreaming, Mary Adair swung her cutlass at the pirate leader, but she was clumsy with this heavy weapon and she fell sprawling, face-down in the sand. Then she felt the weight of a booted foot on her back. Then the sharp point of a blade pricking her neck.

"Yield or die!" cried the young woman. "I'll slice you up and bury you here next to our treasure chest."

"Unhand me!" Mary begged, like a helpless female victim in one of her granny's old-time stories.

The pirates took her prisoner and sailed away in their ship, the *Calico Bass,* looking for treasure wherever they could find it. At first they treated Mary as nothing better than a servant: she peeled vegetables, helped with cooking, polished the silver dishes used by Calico Jack. But soon she and Jack began to feel friendly towards each other. They both liked fancy clothes. When the sea was calm, the two of them would change into flowing silk dresses and lace petticoats that Jack had found on captured treasure ships. Parading around the deck, laughing and chatting, they looked like two elegant young ladies of leisure enjoying a pleasure cruise.

Jack also taught Mary some practical things, such as how to handle swords and guns until she became nearly as skillful as any man. But how could Jack tell if Mary had the nerve to use these weapons in a fight?

"Shoot me," said Jack, pointing at her own heart.

"I can't," Mary protested.

"Shoot me!" Jack insisted. "That's an order!"

Mary took aim with her pistol, squeezed the stiff trigger, and bang! Jack cried out. A bright red stain appeared. Mary stood still, saying nothing. Then the other pirates started laughing uproariously, as Jack tore open her blouse and revealed a protective breastplate of Spanish steel. What looked like blood had spurted from a hidden pouch of red dye.

"Mary Adair, you have passed the pirates' test," cried Jack. "You are one of us now, and we shall call you 'Mary Daring' hereafter."

So Mary joined Jack's carefree band of pirates, signed their book with blood from her own fingertip, and lived as they did.

From Long Island Sound to the Gulf of Mexico, tales were told about her many daring deeds. Some of those tales were true, no doubt, but others seemed more like the wishful dreams she had spun for herself as a lonely little girl.

POCAHONTAS & JOHN SMITH

America's first love story begins like a European fairy tale. *Once upon a time, there was a handsome prince who fell in love with a beautiful princess, and rescued her. . . .*

No, that's not it. Let's try again.

Once upon a time there was a beautiful princess who fell in love with a handsome man who was not a prince but a prisoner, and she rescued him from being brutally executed by her father's guards. The princess was Pocahontas, the man was Captain John Smith, and their story took place in the lush green wilderness called "Virginia," as it looked to early settlers from England.

As a younger man, Smith had traveled far and wide, yet it seems that he wasn't fully satisfied by what he found in exotic places such as Hungary, Turkey or the Ukraine. He dreamed of other, more exciting destinations, somewhere beyond a more remote horizon. So he finally turned his attention away from the old world, and sailed across the ocean to America with a group of men and women who hoped to establish themselves as farmers in one of the new English colonies. After a tiresome voyage they reached reached the American coast in 1607, and named their little settlement "James Fort" to honor James the First of England, their King.

It was not an easy transition. Some of these inexperienced newcomers might have been successful at farming back home, where good crops grew easily in the rich soil of well-made fields; but they lacked most of the knowledge and the tools needed to start from scratch. Here they found dense forests growing to the very water's edge, and an area of swamps that seemed bottomless. Local weather was either uncomfortably cold and rainy or miserably hot and humid. Flies, mosquitoes, and other insects called "no-see-ums" pestered them. Wild animals attacked. After dark, they listened to growling and howling and other terrifying noises. What ravenous, hideous monsters might be lurking unseen among the trees? What heartless savages might be preparing to strike?

The truth is that most of the animals wanted nothing to do with these people, but their own environment had been disturbed, so they complained about it. Bears growled, wolves howled, birds squawked, and wild dogs barked nervously at any unfamiliar sound.

Among the so-called "savages," that is, Native Americans who were already living there long before the whites arrived, reactions were more complicated. Some regarded the European settlers as enemies to be driven away. Others saw them as evil demons to be killed. And a few, including young Princess Pocahontas, were simply fascinated by the sight of these foreign people, many of them blond-haired and pale-skinned, in their peculiar-looking clothes. It was as though dozens of strange gods and goddesses had suddenly appeared, or weird beings from the moon; the thrill of a lifetime!

Captain John Smith stood out from the other English colonists. Bigger, bolder, and more colorful than the rest, he did not enjoy sharing their dull lives. By night he kept watch with some of them, talking about farming and fishing, while secretly hoping for excitement. By day, however, Smith often ventured into the woods alone, seeking what? He wasn't sure.

One afternoon, several miles from the settlement, Smith was captured and disarmed by a group of powerful men who looked as foreign to him as he did to them. Almost naked, dark-skinned, their faces painted to inspire fear, the men tied Smith with leather thongs and led him through the forest to a hidden village. It consisted of wooden huts built around a wide clearing, with a larger ceremonial building at one end. Inside the Indian Chieftain or King sat on a brightly decorated throne, while members of his tribe sat or stood nearby in attendance. Smith, still tied up, had to lie on the dirt floor as everyone regarded him for a long time in silence. Presently the King, whose name was Powhatan, gave a signal, and pointed to the center of the open space, where blocks of stone formed a massive platform.

What happened next was described by Captain Smith himself in a book he completed years later. Several of the King's guards dragged him across the dirt floor and forced him to kneel with his head on one of the stones. They stood "ready with their clubs, to beat out his brains," Smith wrote, when suddenly a loud and melodramatic voice interrupted them.

"Stop! Father, I beg of you, tell them to stop!"

The crowd gasped and drew back, as King Powhatan's daughter, Pocahontas, dashed forward impulsively, pleading with her father to have mercy. The guards, fearful of her anger, hesitated to strike at Smith. But the King impatiently ordered them to go ahead. As people shouted and screamed, Pocahontas threw herself across Smith's body, resting her head on his head.

"Kill me instead!" she cried.

This her father would not do, naturally, so everyone waited to see what was going to happen next. The crowd of onlookers whispered among themselves while Pocahontas sobbed. Smith, bearing her weight on his body, his face wet from her tears, could only guess at what these people were saying. He was torn between discomfort and relief and something else: even in his fantasies of high adventure, seldom had he dared to imagine a scene of such drama and romance; and here it was actually happening!

The King usually granted his daughter anything she asked for. And usually she got bored with it before long. And therefore, Powhatan reasoned, if Pocahontas wanted to amuse herself for a while with this intruder, this pathetic figure dressed in black like a molting crow, why not? She'd soon tire of him, surely, and that would be the end of it. Therefore Powhatan gave an order, servants helped the Princess to her feet, and Captain Smith was quickly untied.

Standing before the King, their hearts beating wildly, Pocahontas and Smith looked at each other with the most intense curiosity. He was struck by her vivid, youthful beauty, her regal bearing, the gleam of passionate interest in her dark eyes. She smiled, sensing his adventurous spirit, much like her own. Thoughts and feelings passed between them like a new language: Freedom! Discovery! Love! Or something like love, at least for this early chapter of their story.

Together they left the King's presence, and wandered to the edge of the deep forest. With no conscious effort they were able to communicate, partly in the language of her people, partly in English, partly by gestures. Smith offered her a piece of ginger candy from his pocket, and she chewed it with pleasure. She showed him where to pick some tasty berries. They agreed to meet again the next day.

Pocahontas was hardly more than a child, Smith gradually realized, and he in truth was not quite the ladies' man he sometimes pretended to be. As the young Princess began to speak enthusiastically but vaguely of adult intimacy, about which she presumably knew very little, Smith didn't want to disillusion her, nor spoil their innocent relationship as it blossomed. So he tried to steer the conversations into other topics. Flowers seemed safe enough. Trees and shrubs. And later animals, starting with their favorite pets. He still missed the border collies he had left behind in England, while Pocahontas apparently had an entire zoo of tame or partially tame creatures at her disposal. She especially enjoyed the amusing antics of a gorgeous blue macaw, which would fly or walk ahead of her in the forest, and do tricks.

Under the watchful eyes of King Powhatan's guards, the Princess and the Captain met often in the woods near Jamestown. They walked, they talked, and during the next two years they tried to educate each other. Smith told Pocahontas a lot of stories about life in England, a little of its history and culture, and some of his exciting experiences in other countries as well; a fascinating mixture of fact and fiction. She taught him the myths of her people, the legends and prayers, and in reponse to his questions, as much as she knew about the lands traditionally occupied by her father's tribe.

As he absorbed the information, Smith was already thinking about "discovering" a lot more of this vast America, and claiming it for England, before other Europeans could get their hands on it. This project gradually seized Smith's imagination so strongly that his earlier thoughts and feelings about Pocahontas seemed to fade away, like morning mists as the sun rises.

With a fond farewell from the blossoming young Princess, and what seemed to be a generous gift of territory from her father, who was glad to get rid of him, Captain Smith sailed north from Jamestown in 1609. He carefully explored the Chesapeake Bay and other coastal areas, which now supposedly belonged to him, thanks to King Powhatan. Continuing northward, Smith took his ship into many of the major rivers and harbors of "New England," which he named and mapped years before the Pilgrims landed there in 1620. And somewhere in the course of those northern voyages, he began to call himself "Admiral" Smith rather than "Captain," as he tried to get credit for his discoveries. He did not return to Virginia.

Pocahontas was only seventeen when John Smith sailed out of her life. She missed him greatly for a while, but as time passed the splendid memories faded; later she fell truly in love and got married to another English settler, one John Rolfe, who promised that he would take her to London.

Several years later he happily did so. Pocahontas, dressed in the lavish costume of an English noblewoman but escorted by some of her father's imposing Indian guards, caused a sensation in the city. Everyone wanted to meet her and every door was open to her, from royal palaces to common taverns. Before long, however, she became severely ill with a disease known as smallpox, and despite the best efforts of the Queen's own physicians, Pocahontas died in her husband's arms at the tender age of twenty-one.

RIP VAN WINKLE

Rupert Van Winkle and his twin brother Ezekiel were the laziest fellows in Kaatskill, New York, a sleepy Dutch settlement on the Hudson River. The brothers had lost their little restaurant business when times were bad, in the 1890s, and they found nothing else to do. Usually they slept through the night and most of the day, only emerging from their untidy cottage at sundown to beg food and drink.

Neighbors would laugh as the two fat brothers waddled along the quiet village street. "Here come Rip and Zip," they'd say. "Who will feed them tonight?"

The brothers continued to live this way until one foggy evening when the village was closed up tight, as though everyone had left to escape a plague.

"What shall we do?" Rip asked Zip.

"I haven't a clue," Zip replied.

They huddled on a park bench near the river, fearful of shadows and unfamiliar night sounds, feeling hungry and hopeless. But after a while they saw something they hadn't noticed before: alongside the village dock, shrouded in mist, an old wooden ship had come to rest. It looked like a Dutch trading vessel from the early days, short and stubby, with a lighted cabin rising high above the hull. Though the ship was tied up securely, its tattered, square-rigged sails were already set, as though for a voyage.

"Shall we try it?" Rip suggested

"Either that or diet," Zip replied.

They crossed a sagging gangplank from the dock, then climbed up narrow steps to the elevated cabin at the stern of the ship, where glowing lamps could be seen through small windows and an open door.

"Captain will give us food," Rip assured Zip.

"He can't be rude," Zip replied.

Entering the warm, cozy cabin, they beheld a round table, crowded with tempting dishes of things to eat. Behind it sat a bald-headed man in a faded silk coat of palest silver. He greeted them courteously, though his strange accent made the words difficult to understand.

"Vellcom gentlemanz, vellcom doo zhip, zuch vondervul ztuffs you vill eet," he said. He pointed to two empty chairs, and after they sat down he seemed to be drifting off to sleep.

"A bountiful feast," said Rip.

"Six dinners at least," Zip replied.

Not bothering to thank their drowsy host, the brothers hungrily attacked the heaping platters of meat, fish, vegetables, desserts. They took frequent sips of a clear beverage that tasted sweeter than honey. And at some point the old vessel was unexpectedly set free, turning into the current of the river, heading south towards the city of New York, though the Van Winkle brothers didn't care.

"A trip in a ship," said one brother, his mouth full of food.

"For Rip and Zip," the other replied.

Around midnight, as full as two fat fellows could possibly get, the brothers fell into big, old-fashioned featherbeds, where they instantly went to sleep. And two days later, yawning and stretching, they awakened on a pier in New York Harbor, surrounded by other sailing vessels much grander than theirs, with blue, white and red banners saying "New Netherlands Festival. 400th Anniversary." Flags of many nations flew from the masts. In the distance were dozens of gleaming buildings that seemed taller than the Kaatskill Mountains. Horseless vehicles roared through the streets, and the noise was incredible.

"What shall we do?" askd Rip.

"I wish I knew," Zip replied.

But their bald-headed host, now awake himself, was there to direct them.

"Hurry, gentlemanz!" he cried.

They climbed aboard an open cart, pulled by big, snarling dogs, which plunged into the terrifying traffic and moved along so rapidly that the wooden wheels hardly seemed to touch the pavement. Skidding to a stop at last, they saw what looked like a bowling green. People in old Dutch costumes, including clumsy wooden shoes and white knee stockings, were practicing a game. Instead of the usual wood bowling pins, however, seven men as fat as themselves stood cowering in the middle of the green, being struck and sometimes knocked down by large wooden balls rolling at them from every direction. Laughter and applause drowned out their plaintive cries of pain.

"Two more here, makes nine," their excited host announced, as Rip and Zip were dragged towards the other fat men. "Now the game beginz!"

"This must be a dream," said Rip.

"So it would seem," Zip replied.

They struggled frantically to wake up, and after many painful moments they did. As they scrambled out of sleep, however, the two fat brothers became separated in time, and neither could return to the year 1900, when their mysterious journey had begun. Rip got safely home, only twenty years after their departure, but Zip missed the starting point by a much wider margin. He went back more than four centuries, landing on a grassy canal bank in rural Holland, to startle and bewilder his stout Van Winkle ancestors.

ROSIE THE RIVETER

Try as she would, Rose O'Farrell could never catch up with her older brother, Gerry. He wasn't that much older, only one year, ten months, and nineteen days; yet he always seemed to be several jumps ahead of her. He was the best speller, the youngest Eagle Scout, the most daring gymnast in Newton, Massachusetts. He excelled at rough-and-tumble football and basketball in high school, while Rosie had to be content with field hockey and cheerleading. At graduation, Gerald T. O'Farrell was voted the "boy most likely to succeed" by his admiring classmates of 1938. Two years later, when Rosie's class graduated, the votes for her were split between "friendliest girl" and "class wit."

With a war coming, Gerry tried to enlist in the Air Force, but found that his football injuries ruled him out. Instead he went right to work in an aircraft factory, as a riveter's apprentice. Two years later, when her turn came, Rosie had to share a job in a flower shop with Fern Feldman, her oldest friend. Fern worked in the mornings, Rosie worked afternoons.

Fern's father, Mr. Feldman, who owned the flower shop, was delighted to have both of the girls working there. "The Fern and the Rose," he used to say, "such a very lovely combination." He took a great interest in the war that was spreading through Europe and Asia, but he was too old for military service himself, so he told the girls and anyone else who would listen that his personal assignment was "to keep their home front beautiful." At this Mr. Feldman proved to be very successful.

Rosie learned to select, trim, and arrange flowers artistically, and delivered them on her way home, since the man who used to do that job was now in the Navy. Rosie had never paid a lot of attention to flowers before, and she was glad to learn how much joy they brought to people who received them: mostly women left behind by men going to war, or elderly couples.

The messages that accompanied the flower deliveries were interesting too. In 1940 they would say things like "Miss you already, I'll get home before you know it." But gradually they changed to "Happy Birthday, Love," or "Happy Anniversary, Darling. Next year we'll be together again."

After a year of this, Rosie could tell that the war was going to drag on for a long time. Her brother would probably be safe now, but she hated the idea that other boys she knew were enlisting or being drafted. Yet it was strangely exciting to meet the ones she didn't know: soldiers and sailors and marines and airmen on their way overseas in fresh, clean uniforms. Rose and Fern would get dressed up after work and go to the USO, the United Services Organization, in Boston. There they could take their pick of hundreds of nice-looking young men in uniform to dance with. Fern preferred the foxtrot, occasionally a tango or a waltz. Rosie loved to jitterbug, swinging higher and higher, until she felt like she was flying.

Then Gerry O'Farrell announced to his family that he had found a way to get into the war after all, driving ambulances for the British army in North Africa. He couldn't enlist with them, but he would probably be allowed to serve indefinitely as an unpaid volunteer. Rosie was suddenly speechless with surprise, while their parents looked both pleased and anxious.

"The recruiter asked me two questions," Gerry recalled with a smile. "Did I have a driver's license, and was I breathing? I told him I'll drive anything on wheels."

"Until that shoulder of yours acts up again," his father said gloomily.

But Gerry O'Farrell could not be discouraged or held back. Two days later, packed and ready to shove off, he gave his sister a big hug and a kiss.

"You going to stick with the flower shop?" he asked.

"I guess," Rosie replied cheerfully.

"Then who's going to fill my shoes?"

"At the aircraft factory?"

"Where else, Sis?" said her brother impatiently. "I'm not talking about the boys' locker room at Newton High."

He was out the door before Rosie could ask him anything else about his old job, but she lay awake for hours that night: wondering, thinking, planning. The next day, before going to work at the flower shop, she took a bus to the busy aircraft factory and located the personnel office. She realized immediately that high heels, a short skirt and a rather tight sweater were big mistakes.

The man behind the desk whistled when he saw her, and grinned wolfishly.

"If great legs could do it, honey, I'd give you any job in the plant, but I have to say this, you just don't look like a riveter to me."

"What does a riveter look like?" Rosie said sourly.

"Come on, I'll show you."

He led her down the corridor to an interior window overlooking the production floor of the aircraft factory. Dozens of workers, many in coveralls, were swarming in and out and around big sections of aluminum wings and fuselages. The screaming noise of high-speed drills and the zipping, thudding sounds of rivet guns were very loud, even through this thick glass.

"Where are the women?" Rosie shouted.

"That's my point," the man replied. "You can't tell which is which here, without a scorecard."

Rosie looked more closely at the busy workers down below. Some wore shapeless beige coveralls; the rest were more or less similarly dressed in drab trousers and shirts. After watching them for a few moments, she began to pick out females by their posture or the way they walked. And some wore eye-shadow, lipstick, small earrings, or red or blue scarves or bandanas on their hair.

"I get the general idea, thank you," Rosie said to the personnel man. "And I will be back," she added to herself. She was glad she hadn't given her name or filled out a job application yet.

After delivering some flowers that evening, Rosie stood before the bathroom mirror at home and wiped every trace of makeup from her face. Her lips were still full and pink, and her eyes still big and blue, but the movie-star prettiness was gone. She took off her dangly earrings and twisted an ugly plaid scarf around her curly red hair.

"That's better," Rosie thought.

Next she went into Gerry's empty bedroom, found a couple of his blue work-shirts, and put one on, tucking it loosely into her baggiest pair of slacks. A pair of white socks, flat-heeled shoes, a shoulder bag to carry lunch, and Rosie was all set to go.

"Now I look like a riveter, I guess. But the next question is, can I learn how to do the job as well as Gerry did it?"

Rosie started working at the factory two days later, after telling Fern and Mr. Feldman the news. She didn't get Gerry's old job, exactly, because for once in her life she could do difficult things that her big brother couldn't have done: crawling inside an airplane's wings, for instance, to line up the holes and drive hot rivets in tight places where only a small-boned person could reach. Within a month, she was no longer just an apprentice. Two months after that she was ready to head a team of three workers, but her supervisor called her aside.

"When are you getting married?" he asked.

"I didn't know I was," said Rosie, puzzled.

"Most girls your age have only one thing on their little minds, kiddo: falling in love, getting married, and raising a family."

"That's more than one thing," Rosie thought, but she calmly explained that she was going to stick with her job for the duration of the war, at least.

"Don't count on it, kiddo," the supervisor said. "Some GI is going to come home and want his job back, sooner or later. Maybe even that hotshot brother of yours."

"Gerry had his legs blown off by a German land mine in

North Africa, and his spine is all broken up," Rosie informed him. "He probably won't be able to walk again. So if you've got no more words of wisdom for me, I'll go back to work."

"I'm sorry. . . ."

Rosie worked grimly for the next year. Her riveting team was usually at or near the top of the list for getting the job done quickly and accurately. The factory produced its one hundredth warplane in May 1944, and Rosie and other workers were to be honored by some distinguished visitors. "Rosie the Riveter," some newspapers had labeled her.

Government officials from Washington asked if they could use a picture of her on recruiting posters. Rosie agreed to that. But when the artist arrived to make sketches, he seemed quite disappointed.

"Rosie the Riveter," he mused. "We were hoping for a sultry brunette, more of what we call a 'calendar girl,' with big brown eyes and Cupid lips; but a patriotic expression, of course. Would you mind if we tried you wearing a wig?"

"Yes, I would mind," Rosie said abruptly. "But I know somebody who might have just what you're looking for."

She scribbled a name and telephone number on a slip of paper, and handed it to the poster artist.

"Here," she said, "And now if you'll excuse me, there's a war on."

Hurrying back to work, she wondered if she should call Fern Feldman to explain what she had done, or let it go. They had been out of touch for the past year or so. She could easily picture Fern posing for the poster, in her place, but how would Fern herself react to this idea? Better call the flower shop right now to find out.

Fern's father answered the phone, and told Rosie that Fern had completed training and gone overseas three months ago, to help the war effort by serving with the Air Transport Command.

"Feldman the Flier," he said proudly. "I'll let her know you called."

★

SWEET BETSEY FROM PIKE

Elizabeth Curry was the prettiest girl in Pike County, Missouri, although she didn't want to be. She wore nice dresses, proper shoes, and hair ribbons because she had to: going to school, going to church, serving tea or orange punch to her parents' guests at home, visiting relatives in St. Louis or Columbia. Whenever she could get free for a while, even if it was just an hour or so in the afternoon, she would quickly change into riding trousers, an old buckskin shirt, and her treasured Indian moccasins. Then she'd put on a well-worn cowboy hat to hide the golden glory of her long hair, as she tried to sneak out of the house.

"Elizabeth!" her exasperated mother would plead with her. "Now just you wait a minute, young lady! Where do you think you'll be going in those outlandish clothes? Are you meeting someone? I don't know what's to become of you, I'm sure."

Betsey didn't know what was to become of her, either, but she usually made some acceptable excuse and slipped through the doorway before her mother could stop her. Outside she'd head for the hill behind the house, where she could gaze in all directions, or she'd walk to the livery stable where she was sometimes allowed to exercise horses. Today she felt like doing both: borrowing a horse, riding it to the very top of her hill, choosing a new destination, and galloping away. But where to? Where should she go? That was always the problem.

Down at the livery stable, Betsey got a surprise. Her best friend, a young man by the name of Ike Henderson, was selling both of his riding horses.

"Headin' to California," Ike explained. "Goin' to buy a wagon and two yoke of oxen, and join this Gold Rush that everybody's been talkin' about."

He was a big, gentle fellow, a few years older than Betsey, with a sweet disposition and something carefree about him, despite his serious expression at the moment.

"You're not really leaving without me, are you?" cried Betsey. "My father says it's only Fool's Gold, as like as not."

For nearly an hour she tried to talk Ike out of going, but his mind was already made up. He had sold most of his belongings, and he would be joining up with a wagon train tomorrow. Betsey finally said good-bye to him and walked slowly homeward, feeling miserable for the first time in her life. She ate no supper and avoided her parents' eyes while she pondered what to do.

The next morning it was Betsey who surprised Ike, climbing aboard his wagon as he was about to hit the trail with the others.

"Don't ask," she said firmly. "I'm eighteen years old, I know what I'm doing, and I am going with you."

At first it was a great adventure for both of them, learning to drive the oxen, cooking their dinners in the open, sleeping at opposite ends of the wagon or out under the stars. Ike's old yellow dog slept between them, his spotted hog kept watch for them all night, and his Shanghai rooster woke them every morning at dawn.

After three or four weeks, however, they were getting tired of traveling. The wagon train creaked along so slowly, day after day, and there was little to discuss with people in other wagons except the weather or, of course, the distant prospect of gold. This seemed like anything but an adventure! Kansas was even flatter than Missouri; when Ike's old yellow dog ran away one afternoon, they could see the dust it raised for miles.

"Dog gone," said Ike with a forced smile, trying to make light of their loss.

Up through the Colorado foothills they toiled, and into the Rocky Mountains, where Ike traded his rooster for a well-used guitar and some lessons. To pass the time away, as they rode along in the wagon, he began writing a song:

"Did you ever hear of Sweet Betsey from Pike? She crossed the wide prairies with her HUM-HUM Ike. . . ."

Betsey looked curiously at Ike, pulled off her floppy sunbonnet, and shook out her thick golden hair.

"What's HUM-HUM?" she asked.

"Whatever you say it is," Ike replied, blushing.

So they were married near Salt Lake City, Utah, by a Mormon preacher, and Betsey continued the endless journey westward with her new husband. After rafting across the wide Platte River, they had to drop out of the wagon train when they lost a wheel. They sold their four oxen to buy supplies. They talked about what to do next.

"Ike," said Betsey, "you and I have found something much more precious than gold. Do we have to walk all the way to California to prove it?"

"No, Betsey, I guess not," her loving husband Ike replied.

They settled near Las Vegas and started a livery stable, which turned out to be quite a good business. They enjoyed every moment of their busy life together. And a golden-haired daughter, born to them the following year, soon became known as the prettiest girl in all of Nevada, though she didn't want to be.

TENNESSEE'S DAVY CROCKETT
GOES TO WASHINGTON

Davy Crockett liked nothing better than a good fight, the way other people enjoyed a little sports activity or just plain exercise. But after he was elected to Congress in 1827 by the voters of western Tennessee, he figured he'd better act more like a gentleman, at least to start with. So Davy bought the largest size of a dignified black suit he could find, cut off some of his tangled hair with a hunting knife, and left his long rifle at home when he set out on foot for the city of Washington, D.C.

He was thinking about politics as he stepped lightly along a narrow trail through the forest, not paying as much attention as he should have. And suddenly he found himself surrounded by fierce Indian braves wearing war paint, carrying tomahawks, and pointing muskets at him.

Fifteen or twenty against one! What a fight that could be! Davy let out a loud cry of joy, startling his captors for a moment, but he didn't attack them immediately because he might have ruined his new clothes. As he hesitated, the crowd parted and another Indian appeared, a man so large that Davy actually felt small by comparison. This man dressed like the other Indians in winter buckskins but he carried no weapons, only a law book that looked familiar to the puzzled backwoodsman.

"Congressman Crockett, I presume," he said, his voice sounding much more refined than Davy's own. "Allow me to introduce myself."

Davy learned that this imposing Indian was a full-blooded tribal chieftain, who used the name Pericles Eubanks when it was necessary for him to deal with whites. He said he had earned degrees in the study of theology and law at Georgetown

College, and now he was back living among his people to help protect their interests.

"Do you intend to represent us in Washington," he asked Davy, "as well as you will serve your own kind?"

Davy was wondering if he could possibly beat this young giant in a wrestling match, just the two of them, but he heard the question and answered yes, indeed. He planned to represent each and every one of the people in his Congressional district.

Eubanks then explained that his tribe had been cheated out of a stretch of land that was traditionally theirs, meaning of course it was theirs to use for now with permission granted by the gods. This land was between the Tennessee River and the Mississippi in Crockett's own district.

"I'd surely get hung if I tried to give any land back to these Indians," Davy thought. "But what the heck? I believe that I'm their Congressman too, so I'll listen."

"Let me have your story," he said aloud.

"In the time before time," Eubanks began, "when He-Who-Is-Sky came down to visit She-Who-Is-Earth. . . ."

Davy tried to interrupt, but Eubanks insisted on telling it in the traditional way. Sky, earth, more sky, torrential rainstorms, lots of loud thunder and lightning, flooding, then lakes and rivers forming, sun shining, more and more people born, people learning how to use the land on which the gods allowed them to live.

"How's that again?" said Davy. "Why right there in your law book. . . ."

"Indian laws are different," Eubanks assured him.

Eubanks escorted Davy Crockett the rest of the way to Rogersville, Tennessee, where he caught the next stagecoach to Washington.

Davy caused a stir in the capital city. President John Adams objected when he tried to camp out on the lawn of the White House, and the few hotels and public boarding houses seemed too crowded and noisy. Davy ended up sleeping on a leaky flatboat anchored in the Potomac River.

Several of the more sophisticated members of Congress used to laugh at him behind his back, and as they got bolder they began to laugh in his face. Davy was fuming angry, but keeping a grip on himself. So far.

"Got to control my temper," he thought. "Those fellows are nothing but skunks and weasels, unworthy of my fists."

The Washington weather got colder and Davy gradually cooled off. He took his seat in the House of Representatives each morning, and did nothing that would call attention to himself. But this only made him feel useless.

"Don't just set there like a stump," suggested an older Congressman who had for some reason befriended him. "Introduce a bill."

"What does that mean, exactly?" Davy asked.

"Write a new piece of legislation about something that's important to you. Show 'em you've got a brain in your head, Congressman Crockett."

Davy considered various subjects and stayed up half the night scribbling his first long speech on pieces of paper that he couldn't read afterwards. The next day, when it was his turn to speak, he got to his feet immediately but stuttered and stammered. Finally he was able to think of something to say.

"In the time before time," he began, "when He-Who-Is-Sky took a fancy to She-Who-Is-Woman. I mean, She-Who-Is-Earth. . . ."

Everybody was laughing at him, even the visitors up in the balcony. Davy struggled for a while, but he got all twisted and tangled in the history of the Indians. So he couldn't prove these people had been cheated out of land that was rightfully theirs. After an hour of listening to raucous insults and loud war whoops from other Congressmen making fun of him, Davy ceremoniously removed his black coat and rolled up his shirtsleeves.

"Would any of the gentlemen care to step outside and debate this matter further?" he asked, mocking their formal Eastern ways. But the others were frightened of him now, and they avoided any discussion of his ideas.

When the Congressional recess began in May 1828, Davy went home to his part of Tennessee for six months, feeling fed up with politics and politicians, more determined than ever to find himself a good fight. And during that long, hot, idle summer, since he had nothing else to do, he found more than a few people to fight with.

Davy did have a brain in his head, however, and when he wasn't fighting physically he gave some serious thought to other things. And so, when he returned to Washington in November, he fought for the rights of people who couldn't fight for themselves, such as poor "squatters" trying to settle on public land in the West. Later he firmly opposed the Indian Removal Act of President Andrew Jackson, though this caused him to lose his bid for re-election to Congress in 1831. "I bark at no man's bid," Davy Crockett told the voters. "I will never come and go, fetch and carry, at the whistle of the great man in the White House. No matter who he is."

They Called Her "Calamity Jane"

Martha Jane Canary may have been born in Iowa or Missouri or Wyoming between 1850 and 1860; nobody seems to know just where or when. Her mother's identity is a mystery too. Her father may have been a soldier who died young, or one who deserted her mother after Jane was born. In any event, whatever the details, it appears that little Jane was abandoned at an early age. She grew up somehow among military families at various army posts out West. From kindly women she learned how to look after herself, and to care for the sick and wounded. From some of the men she learned how to rope a horse, ride, shoot, and fight like fury with her knife or her fists.

When she came to Deadwood, South Dakota, as a young woman, Jane was tall, dark, almost good-looking, very independent, smart about certain things of a practical nature, and capable of holding her own with just about anybody she ran into. She found a job working for a local doctor, and she was reasonably content.

But then she chanced to meet James Butler Hickok, a bold, strapping, handsome man who went by the name of "Wild Bill." He was her equal in almost every way, and she was his. In a more settled time and place, the two of them might perhaps have fallen in love and lived happily ever after. In the violent frontier town of Deadwood, however, this seemed impossible. Every day, sometimes more than once, Bill had to prove how fearless he was. And Jane faced her share of challenges as well.

Though Jane and Bill really liked each other a lot, their tender feelings were rarely allowed to show. Instead of becoming sweethearts they became friends, but also they were competitors, testing their hard-earned skills to see whether he or she could ride faster, drink more, yell louder, or hit a smaller target with a Colt .45 revolver. Usually there was no clear winner between the two of them.

Saturday nights they would roam the streets of Deadwood together, both dressed in buckskins and boots, carrying guns, looking for trouble and often finding it.

One night in 1876, while Jane was visiting an army family she knew in Sioux Falls, Bill went out to eat dinner with his pals at a new saloon. Afterwards they played poker, as usual, and Bill had pretty good luck. But he paid far too much attention to the game, and didn't notice a nervous man standing nearby, looking on. Just as Bill was about to scoop up the pot, this stranger pulled a gun and shot him in the head!

Why? Maybe because of something Wild Bill had said or done that night. Or maybe because of something that had happened years before, when Bill was a U.S. Marshal in Kansas. There's no way to tell. But the poker cards that Bill Hickok held when he died, two aces and two eights, have since been known as "the dead man's hand."

That was the biggest calamity in Jane's unhappy life, at least the biggest we know of. When she got back to town and heard about Bill's death, she went crazy with grief. She would have killed the murderer, but he was nowhere to be found. . . .

A week later, Jane followed Bill's casket to the graveyard with dozens of sorrowful friends and admirers. She wept openly, and remained there after everyone else had left. Then, still weeping, she sprinkled some prairie dust around the plain board that marked his grave, so that maybe his restless spirit would feel more at home in this lonely place. She wanted more than anything to be buried next to him, of course. But no matter how hard Jane tried to use up her life, no matter how recklessly she lived, it took her nearly twenty-seven years to get there.

Jane did her level best to become as wild as Bill had ever been, maybe even wilder. She never refused a bet, a challenge, or a dare. She hunted wolves with the Army scouts, herded cattle with cowboys, pursued fleeing outlaws with hard-riding posses. To make ends meet, she sometimes worked in carnivals doing trick shots with rifles or pistols, and she used the name "CALAMITY JANE" in Wild West shows as far east as Buffalo, New York. One way or another, she earned money when she could, and spent it wherever she happened to be. But Jane's heart was buried in Deadwood, South Dakota, and sooner or later she always returned there. Several times a year she walked out to the edge of town to visit Bill Hickok's grave. Souvenir hunters had stolen the wooden marker bearing his name, but that made no difference to her. And she didn't bring flowers.

As the years passed, Jane began to show her fearlessness in a different way: she took care of people suffering from smallpox and other contagious diseases. In those days, of course, there were few doctors or trained nurses in the Dakotas. So Jane the amateur was always welcome, in spite of her reputation for hard living. And somehow this rough and reckless woman could be gentle and sure of herself with the sick. She continued doing it until bad luck finally caught up with her again, and she died of an infection when she was about fifty years old.

Calamity Jane was buried back in Deadwood beside Bill Hickok, where she wanted to be, and the words that people spoke at her funeral were full of vivid stories about the two of them. What a pair they made!

— ⭐ —

TWO-TOE TOM THE GIANT ALLIGATOR

Two-Toe Tom was a much larger-than-average alligator, living in the marshes near Gulf Shores, Alabama. And how did he get his name? Some folks guessed he had lost two of his toes in a fight, or a trap. Others thought perhaps he was born that way. But most folks never got close enough to find out. Instead, they made up stories about this huge animal: Tom can climb trees like a red rat snake; he can dig tunnels in the mud, from one pond to the next; he can vanish in the time it takes to blink your eye.

And when anything happened to upset them, naturally, they would blame it on him: Two-Toe Tom ate six of my best chickens; Tom swallowed my brand new fishing rod, reel and all; Tom stole my second-best mule. Before long, old Tom was known as the biggest, smartest, meanest, fastest-moving alligator in all of Baldwin County. Hardly anybody wanted to mess with him face to face.

But then things changed, as they usually do. Down in Florida, in the Everglades, a man named "Gator" Johnson happened to hear talk about Two-Toe Tom.

This Gator was a professional hunter. For the right price, cash preferred, he said he would kill or capture any animal that preyed on farmers and their livestock. And Gator specialized in doing alligators. His ramshackle barn was full of alligator jawbones, with long rows of teeth as sharp as bucksaws. Indeed, he could show you scars on his arms and legs where some of those wicked teeth had bitten him. However, the alligators in that part of Florida were ten feet long at most, including their tails. Gator Johnson was ready, willing and able to tackle something considerably bigger than that, so he loaded his wagon with supplies and equipment and headed north.

"Two-Toe Tom," he said to himself as he drove along. "Two big ole tons, more'n likely. I bet he measures fourteen foot if he's an inch! I can't wait to get my hands on that critter!"

Gator crossed the state line into Alabama, and followed a sandy road along the Gulf Coast. Everyone he met had heard of Two-Toe Tom, and a few people claimed to have seen him, but nobody seemed to know exactly where the giant alligator could actually be found. The nearby marshlands were full of shallow ponds, and from what people said, Tom seemed to be living in all of them.

But that didn't bother Gator Johnson one bit. He had to start somewhere, the sooner the better. So he set up his camp near the edge of the largest pond, fed his two mules, and made some sourdough pancakes with huckleberries for his lunch. While they were cooking, he unloaded a small, flat-bottomed boat from his wagon, and dragged it to the water....

Suddenly he stopped. What could be making those big ripples? As Gator looked out towards the middle of the pond, an enormous snout appeared just above the surface, and an eye the size of a baseball glared at him. Gator was much too excited to be scared.

"Fifteen foot, maybe sixteen!" he shouted. "My oh my, ain't you the beauty!"

Say that again?

Two-Toe Tom knew that he had never been described as a beauty before. He was surprised and pleased. Instead of moving closer and grabbing Gator for a quick meal, which he could easily have done, Tom remained still in the water of the pond, savoring this rare moment, almost dozing off. If an alligator could have purred like a contented cat, he would have. His hooded eyes were closed. But he snapped them open again to see that Gator had run over to the wagon for something. Two-Toe Tom wasn't going to wait to find out what this might be.

Instead he slid swiftly through the water to the shore, caught Gator's wooden boat in his great jaws, and crunched it like a fried king mackerel. Half a dozen swallows and Tom had finished eating it.

When Gator came running back, nothing remained to be seen except a few scraps of wood floating on the surface of the pond, and a pair of yellow electrical wires stretching out from the shore towards the middle. Two-Toe Tom was gone.

"Not to worry" said Gator. "We'll smoke him out."

Gator was carrying a small box, similar to the miner's device called a detonator. He connected the ends of the yellow wires to it, and pushed the metal plunger on top.

BOOM! The dynamite he had hidden in his boat exploded in the depths of the pond.

Water sprayed everywhere. Pieces of wood flew up into the air, along with bones and other things that had been buried in the muddy bottom of the pond for a long time. But there was no sign of any alligators, large or small.

For several weeks, Gator Johnson remained on duty in those marshlands of the Gulf Coast, looking around, moving from one pond to another, without finding the slightest trace of old Tom.

"Guess I got him," Gator finally told the farmers and the fishermen.

"Guess you did," they agreed. And they honestly wanted to keep their bargain with him. But since they couldn't afford to pay cash for his services, they loaded up Gator's wagon with baskets of fresh vegetables, and a generous supply of Gulf shrimp packed in ice. They also gave him an extra mule, for good measure.

As Gator drove his heavily-loaded wagon homeward to Florida, he was thinking about his next assignment already, and planning how to handle it. He never looked back, so he didn't see the giant alligator coming quietly behind him down the country road, grinning like a lovesick hound that has found its true master at last.

Unsinkable Mrs. Brown

Like other heroic women and men, Molly Brown appeared on the scene at the very moment when she was needed to perform her famous deed. Unlike most of the others, however, she did not disappear soon afterwards. Loud, somewhat flashy, totally full of fun, Mrs. Brown lingered proudly in the limelight for twenty years or more, telling and retelling her story of how a courageous American female had rescued many helpless passengers from a damaged ocean liner as it was sinking.

Mrs. Brown's opportunity for heroism came when she was middle-aged, or perhaps a bit more. Traveling to Europe early in 1912 without her dear husband, who had pressing business obligations that required him to remain in Colorado, she was pleased to meet a great many of the most fascinating people in London and Paris, and she purchased some wonderfully zany hats and outlandish dresses. A whole lot of them! Now it was April, and time for her to be going home. With seven steamer trunks packed full and labeled, Mrs. Brown took the train from Paris to Cherbourg, France. Awaiting her at dockside there was the *Titanic*, a famous new steamship designed to be fast and unsinkable; its destination was New York.

Mrs. Brown climbed the gangplank slowly, huffing and puffing more than usual, for the irresistible French restaurants and pastry shops had made their contributions to her already plump figure. She firmly promised herself to walk at least a mile a day, around and around the ship's decks, during her voyage.

But first, being Molly Brown, she wanted people to know who she was and what she was about. "People" to her meant absolutely everybody, all of the passengers and all of the crew: Molly simply had to get their attention and win them over. She did this in a number of different ways, according to her own moods. Once or twice, she sang at the afternoon concerts with other passengers, her deep voice just a little louder than anyone else's. At other times she would pray fervently in the chapel. More often, bubbling over with too much energy, she would lead a mob of delighted children in a madcap race or a "scavenger hunt" from one end of the ship to the other. And when she was feeling really feisty, she would take her new Browning .45 automatic pistol to the stern of the liner and empty one clip after another, shooting at oranges or grapefruit or dinner rolls, sometimes, tossed high out over the waves. Flights of opportunistic seagulls would follow the swift *Titanic,* puzzled by the bullet-punctured food that trailed behind it.

At dinner-time each day aboard ship, Mrs. Brown liked to change into a flamboyant gown, usually purple with diamonds or green with rubies, and do something original to her hair. Then she'd entertain her fellow-passengers at the largest table in the first-class dining salon. She'd tell amusing stories about growing up as Margaret Tobin back East, about meeting her future husband out West, about the fascinating characters she and he had encountered in Denver and the mining towns and the Indian country, her stories so very outlandish and funny that even the stuffiest listeners were amused.

After dinner, Mrs. Brown would change her clothes again to go walking around the deck. Because evenings at sea were really cold, she'd start with extra-heavy woolen underwear, silk bloomers, and two jersey petticoats. Then she'd add an ankle-length cashmere dress, plaid golf stockings, high calfskin boots, a man's cap tied with a silk scarf under her chin, and a muff of Russian sable. She tucked her trusty Browning .45 inside the muff, just in case. Over all of this clothing, with the help of a maid, she wore a chinchilla opera cloak that had cost her adoring husband the not inconsiderable sum of $60,000 back in 1910. Wearing so much, she couldn't walk very briskly, but she kept at it gamely until she had done a mile or more.

Molly Brown and other passengers were still walking and

talking on deck one crisp evening when the *Titanic* ran into something with a tremendous crash! It was probably an iceberg, they were later told.

People screamed, bells rang, whistles blew, lights came on all over the ship, and there was terrible confusion among both passengers and crew. The captain's voice could be heard over loudspeakers, urging everyone to stay calm, but soon the "unsinkable" ship was foundering, settling lower in the water, obviously sinking, and people knew it. The captain's voice faded away. Other voices were shouting orders that nobody seemed to follow.

And that's when Molly Brown took charge, getting several lifeboats lowered into the water and many of the passengers secured in them, waving her .45 pistol to back up her loud commands. Women and children went first, except for Mrs. Brown; she refused to leave the sinking ship until it was almost too late. Then she climbed awkwardly down into the last lifeboat, found a seat, gave most of her warm clothing to others who were thinly dressed. After fixing that terrifying scene in her memory, she kept the tired men rowing on and on, another mile, another mile, with prayers, songs, threats, or promises: whatever was needed to overcome the darkness and the sea.

Who Stole Captain Kidd's Treasure?

William Kidd, captain of his own sailing ship, brought a mixed cargo of furniture and household goods from London to New York in 1696. He was an unpleasant-looking man with a quick hot temper, yet he had gained a reputation for honesty, dependability and courage that impressed the merchants of the day. "Kidd delivers," they would say, "if anyone can."

After leaving some official papers at the harbormaster's office, Kidd walked slowly up Broadway towards the inn where he intended to say until his return to England. Lost in thought, he was surprised to find his way suddenly blocked by two British soldiers in red coats. An officer stepped forward to greet him.

"Captain Kidd? I am Colonel Livingston. His Excellency the Governor wishes to see you at once."

This seemed to be more of an order than an invitation, so Kidd obediently followed the Colonel to the large red brick building that housed the royal governors of this British colony. Governor "Belly" Bellamont, a distant relation of England's King William, was just completing an enormous meal: either a very late lunch or a very early dinner. Now, shoving the empty dishes aside before his servants could remove them, Bellamont spread a map on the table and pointed his fork at the middle of it.

"Nova Scotia," he bellowed. "Part of Canada. Ever been there, Kidd?"

"It is said to be the haunt of pirates," Captain Kidd replied cautiously.

"Precisely, Kidd, precisely," the Governor snapped. "Those godless, lawless, bloody scoundrels! They seize our cargoes, sink our ships, then sail away to Canada and hide their loot on some confounded island."

"Why do you ask me about it?" Kidd wondered.

"We have a proposition for you," the Governor replied. "Tell him, Livingston."

As Bellamont consumed his second chocolate dessert, the Colonel explained to Kidd that a group of British investors wished to arm a suitable ship and send it north to recover stolen property from the pirates in Canada. Other pirates might also be captured along the way. A trustworthy commander was needed and Kidd, they thought, would be just the man for this job.

"But I have a vessel of my own," Kidd objected, "and contracts with merchants back in England. I sail in a week's time."

"You will have some unexpected difficulty with your clearance papers, I imagine," said Livingston, smiling unpleasantly. "Your ship might have to remain tied up here, month after month."

"You can't do this to me," Kidd shouted angrily.

But their stony looks and their silence told him that they probably could. Later that evening they forced him to sign his name to a lengthy document he wasn't even allowed to read.

"Never fear, Kidd," the Governor assured him. "His Majesty has graciously agreed to invest some of his own funds in this new venture, and you will sail as a privateer with his royal pennant flying from your mast."

A "privateer" in those days was a heavily armed ship, privately owned, with a special government license to seize certain kinds of property from certain other vessels. Captain Kidd had no desire to embark on such a business, but he felt trapped now, so he decided to make the best of it. He inspected the investors' ship, supplied it for a voyage that might last a year, and assembled a crew of hardened ruffians and rejects from the Royal Navy. They were misfits, most of them, but he knew how to make them do his bidding, and the ship was soon ready for departure.

Leaving the dock at last, getting back to sea, Captain Kidd had a momentary sense of freedom. As he sailed north from New York, however, his fierce anger rose again. His life was in ruins, his future nothing to look forward to! Having nobody else to take it out on, he bullied his crew day after day, and he ordered them to attack any foreign ship that crossed his path, whether it was actually under the command of pirates or not. One after another, many vessels were captured in this way. Innocent men were killed, or thrown overboard, women and children were mistreated, and cabins were looted for gold, silver, jewels. The year that Kidd had expected to be away became two years, then three.

Finally he wearied of this strange life, and made arrangements to meet the Governor's men secretly at Montauk, New York, near the tip of Long Island. Kidd was rowed ashore with four big treasure chests, which he turned over to Colonel Livingston.

Having done his best to satisfy those who had hired him, the Captain assumed he was finished with them. But when he returned to London later, he was immediately arrested and charged with numerous acts of "piracy on the high seas." Some of the men who had originally invested in his venture now testified against him, to cover their own tracks.

Captain Kidd, having no defense, remained silent. He was quickly found guilty, and executed by hanging on May 23, 1701.

---⭐---

WIND-WAGON THOMAS

Thomas O'Bannion was a saltwater sailor from Ireland, like his father and grandfather before him. He loved the boundless freedom of the ocean, the sky, the winds; it was hard for Thomas when his ship finally reached its destination, where he had to go ashore while cargo was unloaded, repairs made, and supplies carried aboard for the next voyage.

Walking aimlessly through the crowded streets of Liverpool or Hong Kong, Oakland or Valparaiso, he felt little interest in what he saw, and he could hardly wait to escape the limited horizons of city life.

But one day in New Orleans, he happened to meet another young man, as bright and adventurous as Thomas himself, who talked enthusiastically about wanting to build a lot of "flatboats." They were small wooden barges, pulled by mules or pushed by men with long poles, that were just right for inland waters such as the shallow western rivers that feed into the Mississippi. This young man, by the name of Leo Schultz, was looking for a partner to help him get rich.

"We'll put wheels on flatboats," he declared, "so they can be used as wagons as well, and then we'll sell them to all those Easterners who are so darn eager to go west." This was right after the beginning of the "gold rush" of the 1850s, when people were heading for California by ship, wagon, horseback, or on foot.

"When they get there," Leo continued, "they can take the flatboats apart and use the wood for houses."

He filled in the rest of his plan so confidently that Thomas agreed to join him in this project, even if it meant turning away from the sea for a month or two.

The next morning, Thomas and his partner caught the

stagecoach for Kansas, where they could build some "flatboat wagons" and sell them to Easterners crossing the Missouri River. As they traveled farther into the open country, Thomas was surprised to find that he was starting to like it. Later, when he could see vast stretches of prairie ahead, with the wind making waves through the grass, he felt as though he had almost gone back to sea. Not so bad here after all!

At a town called Westport Landing, Kansas, Thomas and his partner bought lumber and wagon wheels. Neither of them knew much about doing carpentry, but their design seemed simple enough: a flat, rectangular box made of sturdy wooden planks resting on two long beams. The hardest part was attaching the wheels so that they could turn freely without coming loose. Thomas tried to do it with bits of rope, which didn't work.

"Why don't we just give people the four wheels," Leo said impatiently, "and let them figure it out?"

Then along came someone from Charleston, South Carolina, who showed them how to carve wooden axles for the wheels. Problem solved. Soon they had four completed, and their first flatboat wagon was ready to sell.

Thomas and Leo put up signs on this side of the river and also on the far side, where the overland trail to the west began at the water's edge. They waited for customers. A few people stopped to look, but nobody wanted to buy. They lowered the price, and lowered it again. Still no sale. The two young partners were getting discouraged.

"I like your basic idea," one man said, "but I just can't afford it. You know, the cost of horses and mules is sky-high right now, and it would take at least two of them to pull that thing."

So Thomas and Leo reluctantly decided to go out of business. All they had to do was remove the wheels from their flatboat wagon, find a suitable cargo, and float it down the river to New Orleans. There they could deliver the cargo, sell the flatboat, and maybe the wheels, and Thomas could go back to sea.

At the very last minute, however, standing near the river

with a brisk breeze blowing, Thomas had a better idea.

"We don't need horses or mules to pull this thing," he said. "All we have to do is add a mast and a sail."

Leo was doubtful, but Thomas persuaded him to try it. With the last of their money, they bought a white oak tree and trimmed it for the mast, a smaller one for a boom, and several used canvas tents from which they could stitch together one sail. Then all they had to do was add some ropes for the rigging, and a fair number of heavy stones for ballast, and the world's first "wind-wagon" was ready to go!

Thomas and his partner jumped aboard, hoisted the new sail, and caught an evening breeze blowing west from the river. Once they were clear of the willow trees along the riverbank, the wind-wagon gained speed, and soon they were racing across the smooth, flat, seemingly endless prairie towards the setting sun. Thomas was so excited that he completely forgot about trying to steer the wind-wagon or slow it down. Straight as a seabird they flew with the wind from the east, hour after hour, until at last their speeding wagon crashed into the purple foothills of the Rocky Mountains, more than a thousand miles from their starting point. From there they decided to walk the rest of the way to California, and they never came back.

THE WORLD'S BUSIEST BUCCANEER

Jean Lafitte was once the busiest buccaneer in his part of the world, and some would say the most successful. In the early 1800s he seized more than a hundred rich merchant vessels, squeezing millions of dollars out of them. He did so by selling nearly everything he stole: cargoes, cannons, the ships themselves, sometimes even their surviving crews and their passengers, in the lawless ports of the Caribbean Sea. Lafitte's treasure chests, stuffed with gold and silver, were buried on Caribbean beaches or on outer islands from the Bahamas to Texas, and mostly forgotten. If Lafitte made any maps or records of the exact locations, they were lost when he died. During his lifetime, however, he seems to have kept his greedy followers loyal to him by handing out small shares of treasure every once in a while, and promising more.

To celebrate his successes, Lafitte liked to visit the city of New Orleans occasionally. There he felt at home among the French-speaking people. He would stroll through the gayest streets without any escort, splendidly dressed in stolen finery, and give away his pocketful of coins as he pleased. Many people welcomed him, because of his boldness and generosity, though some of the city's officials took a different view. Lafitte was a criminal, after all, who should be brought to justice for his countless crimes.

But this was a lot more easily said than done. At one point, Governor Claiborne of Louisiana posted a $500 reward for his arrest. When Lafitte heard about this, he put up his own notice, offering a much larger reward for the arrest of the Governor! Nobody took Lafitte's offer seriously except Claiborne himself, who promptly sent gunboats up the coast to capture the bold buccaneer in his stronghold, the fortified village of Barataria. Like similar efforts in the past, this one met with no success.

Jean Lafitte might have continued his carefree life of crime indefinitely if fate had not intervened. In 1812, the British government decided to try again to recapture its former colonies, now the United States of America, so a war started. One of its principal targets was New Orleans, from which the Mississippi River and much of the interior of the new nation could be controlled. A number of battles were fought, but the American navy and the coastal defenses were not overcome. After two years of failure, the frustrated British admirals devised a new scheme: they would give military rank and other inducements to the notorious buccaneer, Jean Lafitte, if he and his followers agreed to come into the war and fight on Britain's side.

What the British didn't know, evidently, was that Lafitte hated their country because of how it had defeated France, his native land, in the European war recently ended. Now he saw an opportunity to do the armed forces of Britain great harm. From his stronghold at Barataria, Lafitte sent a detailed letter to his old enemy, Governor Claiborne, outlining the British plans and saying he would rather fight on the American side.

"I am the stray sheep wishing to return to the fold," Lafitte assured the Governor. "I will help Louisiana in any way I can."

Believe a pirate? Claiborne wondered if he should. He talked with Andrew Jackson, the commanding general of the American forces, then invited Lafitte to join them.

In the spectacular battle that followed, a fleet of British warships fired their long-range cannons at theAmerican forts all day and all night. The forts fired back, but most of the gunners now were Lafitte's men. French and Spanish and Dutch and who knows what other nationalities, their aim was deadly after years of experience as buccaneers.

Bam! Ba-blam! Bam! Bam! The American guns roared.

One after another, British frigates exploded or burned and sank, until the remainder of the fleet withdrew in defeat.

A short time later, news from Washington, D.C. reached the joyful residents of New Orleans. Peace had been declared! In fact, the war had officially ended before this battle had started, but that didn't stop the excited citizens from celebrating loudly, and expressing their gratitude to Jean Lafitte.

Music filled the air; people in carnival costumes were everywhere, dancing and singing. Lafitte, their hero, made speeches on the same public platforms with Governor Claiborne and General Jackson, who soon grew tired of hearing him talk.

And there was more news: the President of the United States had recently issued an order, giving Captain Jean Lafitte and his men full pardons for any crimes they had committed, up to January 8, 1815.

Most of the buccaneers decided to come ashore for good at that point, either to live more quietly as smugglers in the Louisiana bayous, or to retire as law-abiding citizens. Lafitte himself tried to do likewise, for a while, but he gradually realized that the quiet life was not for him.

He returned to buccaneering, like other famous outlaws in American history, because he honestly couldn't think of anything else to do.

YELLOW-EYED GOAT SEES RED

Hector Hardscrapple worked at a tire and rubber factory near Philadelphia. For nine hours a day, six days a week, Hector packed new automobile tires into cardboard cartons to be shipped to garages and gas stations around the country. It was an easy job that left him with plenty of time for his own thoughts, yet Hector was ready to make a change. What he really wanted was to be a farmer, as his father had been. During his lunch hour, while other workers were talking or resting, Hector would study the "Farms for Sale" ads in the newspaper, and think about having a place of his own.

This was during the early 1930s, when times were hard for most people. The prices for small pieces of agricultural real estate were dropping lower and lower, but they were still too high for Hector. He didn't have a lot of money saved up, so he kept on reading the ads until finally he found a Pennsylvania farm listed for five hundred dollars "as is." It had a house, a barn, some woods, and eighty acres that had been cleared of trees and brush to grow crops.

After work, Hector made a long-distance phone call to find out more about the place. Then he hurried home to tell his wife, Harriet. She thought maybe it sounded a little too good to be true.

"What's the catch?" was her first question.

"Well, it's quite a long ways from here," Hector replied. "About twenty miles the other side of Scranton. Back up in the hills, kind of."

"Up in the mountains, you mean. What else?"

"Well, the soil is probably kind of stony...."

"And?" Harriet demanded.

"And it seems there's a railroad track running right

through the middle of it. But the place comes with some live-stock," Hector added hastily. "Four dozen hens, a rooster, a couple of plow-horses, two cows for milk. And a goat. We could make a living there, honey."

Harriet said nothing more for the moment. She was a farmer's daughter herself, and she knew how difficult it could be for two people to make a decent living, even on the best of farms. But she also knew her husband: Hector had his heart set on getting back to the land. She understood this feeling, of course, so she talked the whole thing over with him that night, and finally they agreed to try it.

Hector gave her a great big hug. "Harriet, you'll never re-gret this," he assured her. "If anybody can make a go of the place, we can."

"You may just be right," Harriet replied. "You're the stub-bornest guy that I ever heard of, and I'm pretty good at making ends meet, so we'll see what happens."

After the first month or two, Hector and Harriet both felt that they had made the right choice. Their house was small but snug, and freshly painted. The barn looked almost new. The chickens laid plenty of eggs, large tan ones with brown speck-les, and Harriet soon had a list of regular customers from the little town nearby, people who would rather not buy their eggs in a store. Also, the land was not quite as stony and barren as she had feared. Hector plowed three fields and planted his first crop of sweet corn. At night he read "how to" booklets about new techniques of farming from the county agricultural office. Harriet was glad to see him looking so contented.

Hector worked six days a week and almost never com-plained. On the seventh day, however, he liked to rest and go to church with Harriet. He usually wore a red silk shirt that she had given him for his last birthday. Wearing it was his way to show the world that going to church meant something special to him.

One Saturday afternoon in September, Harriet carefully washed Hector's red shirt and hung it outdoors so that it would be dry the next day. A nice breeze snapped the fabric, making the shirt wave back and forth like a large red flag. Soon it caught the attention of the big yellow-eyed goat that had lived on the farm for years. This stubborn animal was quite self-satisfied, more or less useless, and somewhat mysterious to Hector, who had never owned a goat before.

The goat evidently liked red-colored things better than anything else in the world: red apples, the covers of Sears Roebuck catalogs, empty ketchup bottles, rusted Campbell's Soup cans, whatever he happened to find. He spotted things, he picked them up, and they quickly disappeared. Did he eat them, or just bury them somewhere on the farm? Hector was'nt sure.

But this time, as he looked out the kitchen window, Hector actually saw the goat rear up on his hind legs, grab the red shirt in his teeth, and yank it down from the wash line, taking clothespins and all. Then the goat started swallowing his shirt! Hector put down the fried egg sandwich he was eating, and ran out of the house.

"Let go of my red shirt, you stupid cuss!" he shouted. But the goat paid no attention, and continued to swallow one of the shirt's long sleeves, little by little by little, as though he had never tasted anything half so good.

"Let go, let go!" Hector grabbed the end of the other sleeve before it vanished, and tried not to tear his shirt as he pulled. But this goat was surely the very stubbornest of the stubborn: he dug in his feet, he kept on swallowing, and soon there was nothing left to be seen, except for a few red threads between the goat's front teeth.

Harriet came running from the chicken house when she heard the fuss.

"Hector, it's all right," she said. "I've got some extra money saved up, from selling eggs. I'll buy you another red shirt."

But for Hector it wasn't all right. He wanted his own shirt back, period. And if he couldn't have it, this blankety-blank son of a billy-goat wasn't going to enjoy it either!

That was the whole story right there!

So Hector cut a piece of rope from the clothesline, put a loop of it around the goat's neck, and started dragging him across the farmyard. Naturally the goat reacted by trying to plant all four of his feet, but Hector was strong and angry, so the two of them moved off slowly towards the woods.

"Hector Hardscrapple," his wife cried. "Whatever are you doing? You're surely not going to hang that poor animal?"

"Hanging's too good for him," Hector yelled back. "I'm going to teach him a lesson he'll never forget, if he lives long enough to remember it."

Harriet followed at a distance behind them, as Hector slowly dragged the reluctant goat through the woods to the single railroad track that cut across the middle of their farm. A train whistle sounded in the distance; they were just in time for the afternoon freight.

Using his rope, Hector quickly tied the goat across the track where the train would be sure to hit him. The goat tried to resist, of course. Hector added an extra knot, and then another one, just in case.

"Oh, Hector, you can't do this," Harriet protested, but Hector wasn't about to give up now.

"Teach him a lesson he'll never forget," Hector repeated, panting with effort. "I can be stubborn too."

He waited until the freight train was getting pretty close, then turned his back on the goat and walked away.

"Hector?" his wife pleaded.

"Nope," said Hector. "My mind is made up."

Meanwhile the goat, tied to the track and seeing a train coming right at him, was able somehow to cough up most of Hector's red shirt. With the rest of it still gripped in his teeth, he swung his head back and forth as hard as he could.

The man driving the train leaned out of a side window in the locomotive, and caught sight of what appeared to be an emergency signal flag, bright red for danger, waving on the track ahead. He slammed on the brakes and the train squealed to a stop, just inches short of hitting the goat.

Hector looked back, saw what was going on, and ran to

get his shirt before anything else could happen to it. Except for a small tear in one sleeve, it looked all right.

"This your goat?" asked the train driver.

"Yes, but I've been thinking about getting rid of him," Hector replied.

"I can see that, sure enough," the driver said. "Would you possibly be interested in getting rid of him a different way?"

"How do you mean?" said Hector cautiously.

"Well, the thing of it is, I've always wanted to have a high-spirited animal like yours for a pet," the driver explained. "I couldn't pay you any money for him, I'm afraid, but I might be able to trade you something. Let's see. How about. . . yes, how about this pair of red suspenders I'm wearing?"

"Let me think a minute."

Hector examined the red elastic suspenders with considerable interest, and naturally the goat did too. Hector thought those suspenders would look really good with his red shirt, but he didn't know what the goat might be thinking.

There was a long moment of silence on the track, with steam hissing softly from the engine of the waiting train. Then the goat turned his head towards Hector, looking up at him, and Hector looked straight back into the animal's deep, fearless yellow eyes.

Something happened. . . .

"I don't know," said Hector. "How about I trade you the shirt for your suspenders, and I keep the goat?"

"All right by me," the train driver replied. "I sure do like that shirt."

"I like it myself," said Hector. "In fact, I'm thinking that maybe I've come to like it just a little bit too much."

So Hector Hardscrapple gave the red shirt to the train driver, put on his new pair of red suspenders, untied the rope, and led his yellow-eyed goat home to the farmyard. There he found Harriet standing beside the clothesline, cheerfully hanging up a clean white shirt for him to wear to church the next day.

Acknowledgments & Credits

The cover image for *Uncle Sam's Family* is a photograph of a 19th century weathervane in the collection of the Smithsonian American Art Museum, Washington, DC, unknown artist, catalogued as "Horse and Uncle Sam Driver." Accession Number 1966.45. Used by permission. Thanks to Dr. Elizabeth Broun, Director of the Museum. Book cover design by Tatiana Vila. The image of Uncle Sam walking, from wpclipart.com, is in the public domain. Text formatted by Maureen Cutajar. Earlier versions of these stories were included in *American Folk: Classic Tales Retold*, published by Harry N. Abrams, Inc., text copyright 1998 by Charles Sullivan. Thanks to the late Paul Gottlieb, publisher and friend, for this and much else.

About the Author and His Other Books

Charles Sullivan, born in Massachusetts, has lived, studied and worked in approximately 30 different U.S. zipcodes, plus foreign countries, before settling down in California. He is the author and editor of numerous books for adults, teenagers, and younger children. Go to www.charlessullivanbooks.com for titles, descriptions, and book reviews. His other interests include history, education, public service, the environment, and boating. For further information about Sullivan's varied career, see *Who's Who in the World*.

Contact Information

Email the publisher: kezaco@earthlink.net. Telephone (415) 362-2262. Or fax (415) 474-4544.

Copyright & License Notices

Author's Bonus to the Reader

Included for you to read in this ebook *Uncle Sam's Family* is a sample of four poems, copyright 2012 by Charles Sullivan. These poems try to capture some of the personal stories from which folk tales may later arise. To read more of Sullivan's poetry, look for the ebook *Santa Fe Voices,* which is currently scheduled for publication early in 2013.

Poem from *Santa Fe Voices*, copyright 2012 by Charles Sullivan

BEAR TALK

You've been sprawling
on these matted weeds and grasses
near the river. And I can tell
what you've been eating here,
elderberries and horsetails
and green apples gone wild,
and anything slower than you
that was moving on four legs.
You're busy building fat, like me,
before you go back into the hills
to hibernate. I know this
without words. Today I seem
to be some kind of a bear myself,
not as broad or heavy as your tracks
say you are, but fiercer I hope,
in case we ever meet.

MAN WITHOUT GUITAR

Ran out of gas
as I sometimes do,
and couldn't find
but a dollar forty
under the seat,

nickels and dimes
and three of those new
galvanized quarters,

so I'm walking home
with holes in my boots
and it's starting to rain
as it sometimes does,
drops of different sizes
like small change.

VILLAGE POLITICS

The owner of the grocery store came to see me. Mister Busy-Body is his name.

"This village needs a new mayor," he said. "The job has been vacant since August 23rd of last year. It doesn't take much time, the way I see it, so it doesn't pay much."

"I'm no politician," I said.

"You're the fattest guy around," he said. "If there was ever any trouble about money or such things, you couldn't leave in a hurry."

"That figures," I said. "People aren't likely to trust a skinny guy."

"Not after the last one," he said.

"I'll think it over," I said. "I'll talk to my wife and get back to you. Soon as I finish my lunch."

Poem from *Santa Fe Voices*, copyright 2012 by Charles Sullivan

WOMAN FROM ACOMA

In those days,
she said, our *pueblo*
was known as Sky City.

Every house on the mesa
had its own special ladder.

When warm weather came,
people would sit together
on the roofs late at night,
talking with neighbors,
reading the stars for news
or entertainment.

In those days the great
constellations had names,
personalities, and their stories
were constantly changing;
you couldn't just lie back
and go to sleep, thinking
"I've seen that one before."